USA TODAY Bestselling Author

PENNY WYLDER

This is a work of fiction. Names, places, characters and incidents are either products of the author's imagination or used fictitiously and any resemblance to actual persons, living or dead, or businesses, organizations, or locales, is completely coincidental.

ISBN-13: 978-1984135797
ISBN-10: 1984135791

Chapter 1

I haven't seen Lily Saxon in almost two years. After college, I stayed up by Atlanta for my job, and she came down here, two hours south to Columbus for hers. Close enough that we should be able to see each other, far enough away that it's not easy or convenient. Just one of those things…girls who are your best friends can suddenly disappear. We've tried to keep in touch, even though neither of us are particularly good at it. Which is why I was ecstatic when I found out she was finally getting married to the guy she's been gushing about for three years. And which is also why my jaw dropped when I entered this church.

The building itself is gorgeous, an old building with all the little details of something that was built in the past. Carved wood and high, arching windows. The colors of the wedding are a sensuous crimson and black, which gives the atmosphere an air of mystery and an edge of darkness that you don't usually associate with weddings. But that's not the biggest surprise. There's a sign at the door with a small statement, the same one that was on the invitation that I hadn't given a second thought to.

This is a non-traditional wedding. Please be aware that some guests and members of the bridal party adhere to an alternative lifestyle, and that everything that takes place is consensual.

I honestly didn't think about what that meant until right now, when I walked into the church and the first thing I saw was a woman in a corset, tights, heels, and not much else, being led on a leash by a man in a suit. *What the fuck?*

There's a table for gifts, and I hand mine to the girl standing behind it—young and wearing a low-cut crimson dress. I'm guessing she's a bridesmaid, though I haven't met her before. I don't think anyone from college is in the bridal party, though I think I'll see some of my other classmates in the audience. There aren't any ushers to walk you to your seat, and when I walk into the main space, I can see why. They've rearranged the sanctuary into a circular seating arrangement—all the chairs are surrounding the altar so there's no division between the guests and the bride and groom.

That doesn't mean that the guests aren't divided. On one side of the circle are people dressed normally, sitting in chairs and waiting. On the other side is the distinctly non-traditional part of the wedding. In the front row are men in suits, sitting in the chairs, and barely dressed women sitting or kneeling at their feet. They're covered everywhere that matters, but it still looks like they're wearing lingerie.

There are others, outfits featuring leather and latex and things that I would never consider wearing in public. I'm all for non-traditional, but I'm not sure why these people are here. I guess they might be friends of the groom? But the Lily I knew in college would have been embarrassed just by looking at that side of the circle.

Looking at them is unsettling. They're so comfortable that you almost don't notice the strangeness of their dress and posture, until you do. Even though looking at them gives me a strange, tingling feeling like I've forgotten something, I can't seem to look away.

One of the men sitting in the front row strokes the neck of the woman sitting at his feet, his fingers brushing the metal collar that she's wearing. In response, she leans into his touch, the motion smooth and sensual like a cat, gathering pleasure from his touch. He's looking at her like she's the most precious thing in the world, and she's smiling even though he can't see her. I'm suddenly blushing, because I know that I'm looking at something far more intimate than a touch on the neck should be.

I realize that I'm staring, and that there are people waiting behind me to enter the sanctuary. Yanking my gaze away from the couple, I sit down somewhere between the two sides of the circle and check my phone just for something to do, and to keep myself from staring. Lily sent my invitation with a plus one, but I don't have a plus one at the moment, and I couldn't even think of anyone I wanted to take. Talk about depressing.

I look around, taking note of all the details. Bouquets of crimson and black roses and lilies line the sides of the aisle, and wrought iron candelabras are placed around the central altar and in-between the seating. The result is an intimate atmosphere with a sensual twist. It’s not what I would have predicted Lily would choose, but at least the wedding is beautiful even if it isn’t traditional. Though now that I’m here, I’m wondering if the ceremony is going to be something other than I’m expecting, too.

The seats fill up more, the division between the guests becoming more and more apparent, and finally, right on time, the music starts. There’s a string quartet where the altar would usually be, and the music fills the space perfectly. Everyone turns to face the central aisle as the first of the bridesmaids enters. She’s dressed in a gorgeous off-the-shoulder slinky black dress touched with lace that matches the flowers, and I do a double-take at the metal collar that she’s wearing around her neck. It’s just like the one the kneeling girl is wearing.

The next bridesmaid has cuffs around her wrists. What on earth is happening here? A dawning sensation reaches me that in the two years since I've seen Lily, life may have taken a different path than I thought. Like full on kinky, and by the time the last bridesmaid appears, I'm prepared to see her in full-on bondage gear.

I'm so relieved to be wrong. Lily appears in a white gown, no strange additions in sight, and the minute she sees her fiancé—Mark—at the altar, she transforms into a person so happy and so beautiful I almost don't recognize her. There's a pang in my chest. I want someone who will make me that happy. I want someone that I want so much that I have a smile that looks like it's going to crack my face in half.

The wedding is simple and proceeds much the way I expect it to, until it doesn't. Lily and Mark say their vows, they exchange rings, and then Lily kneels in front of Mark like it's the most natural thing in the world for her to do. Mark steps behind her, placing a simple silver necklace on her and fastening it, all the while murmuring words that are not loud enough for the guests to hear.

I feel stunned more than anything. Glancing over at the 'non-traditional' audience shows that many of them are close to tears, and Lily is too. She looks almost happier than when she spoke her wedding vows. Is this what her life is now? Is Lily one of those women you read about in books who like to get tied up and beaten during sex? Even though we haven't spoken in a long time, I knew Lily really well. I still feel like I know her really well, and the look on her face is genuine happiness. She's not being forced into this. Am I okay with that? Can I be happy for my friend when she participates in something that many people consider abuse?

My gut churns with uncertainty, and I make up my mind to ask her at the reception. If I get to talk to her, I'll be able to know whether she really wants this. And if she does, then I'll do my best to be happy for her. If not, I'll find a way to get her the hell out.

Lily stands, the minister pronounces them man and wife, and the whole audience cheers as they retreat up the aisle to a song that's cheerier than you'd expect at a wedding that's full of crimson and black.

Well, one thing's for sure. This is going down as one of the strangest weddings I've ever been to, and I haven't even gotten to the reception yet.

Chapter 2

It's late by the time I get to talk to Lily. You never actually get to talk to people in a receiving line. It's kind of like an assembly line. After fifteen seconds and a hug, I half expect a woman with a stern face and clipboard to say that we're slowing down production.

So instead, I talk to the people at my table, I eat some of the food —which is delicious—and I drink. I'm learning a hell of a lot more about the scene than I ever knew before, because one of those couples sitting in the front row is at my table. The woman was sitting on the floor and I definitely wasn't doing a good enough job at *not* staring.

Frankly, I'm still not doing a very good job, because I can't dismiss the tiny, nagging feeling that I'm missing something whenever I look at them. Thankfully this couple has been kind about it. They aren't the couple I was watching in the sanctuary, but they behave much the same. And talking to them—both of them—is an experience I'm not going to forget soon.

And now I know that Mark—Lily's now husband— is a Dom or Dominant, and Lily is his sub. Which just blows my mind. Lily was practically afraid of men in college, to the point where I would have to drag her out of our dorm rooms on weekends so she could have some social interaction. But even though this is all new to me, Jenny and Christopher are making me feel a whole lot better about this. Jenny doesn't seem like she's some beaten down woman who does whatever Chris says. In fact, they seem like they have a really solid relationship. I'm relieved.

They told me a little bit about how Lily and Mark met, and that Mark is one of the best men that they know. So when I finally manage to catch Lily alone, I feel prepared.

"Hi!" she squeals, enveloping me in a hug that's full of white tulle. "I'm so happy you could come. How are you? I've been trying to get over here for like an hour but you know weddings. Everybody wants a piece of the bride."

I hug her back. "I'm good. I spent that hour talking to Jenny and Christopher. Or should I call him Master Christopher?" I raise an eyebrow.

She makes an exaggerated cringe. "Yeah. I'm sorry. I didn't know how to tell you about Mark and our lifestyle. It's not easy for people to understand, and they make assumptions. Since we haven't seen each other in person in such a long time…I honestly wasn't sure how you'd react."

I swallow, and take a deep breath, trying to calm the lingering doubts I have. "It's a surprise. I would never have guessed based on the way I had to force your ass to socialize."

"That's true," she laughs. "But it turns out that I just had to find my tribe. It was where I least expected it."

"But…this," I say. "You want this? You're not being forced into it or anything?"

Lily smiles at me in a way that lets me know that she's answered this question probably a thousand times, and maybe several hundred of those times have been tonight. "I understand why you're asking. Believe me, I do. But please believe me when I say that I am happy. Mark is a good man and he would never hurt me. Our relationship—our dynamic—is based on trust and love. I would never do anything I'm not comfortable with, and Mark would never make me."

I still have that little niggling doubt in the depths of my stomach, but she's not lying. Truth and happiness are radiating from her like she's the damn sun, and I find myself getting a little teary. "I'm really glad that you're happy."

"Oh, Emma," she pulls me into another hug. "You're going to be happy too. I just know it. You're going to get everything that you've ever wanted."

Someone taps her on the shoulder and she's swept away into another conversation, leaving me alone wondering what the hell I actually want. *Not this*, my mind instinctively says. Not loneliness, not looking at people who tie each other up and being *jealous* for god's sake. I turn to go back to the table and find Jenny and Christopher locked in a passionate kiss, and I have to look away. Why the hell didn't I come to this wedding with a date? Nothing is worse than being alone at a wedding where everyone is coupled up but you.

I don't go back to the table. I go to the bar and refill my drink. And after that drink, I have another. And another until I'm not feeling sorry for myself anymore and am suddenly feeling sexy and available. This is much better.

"I hope you're drinking water with all of those," a deep voice says behind me. I turn to find an attractive man towering over me, an eyebrow raised as he looks at my drink.

"Last time I checked," I say, "water doesn't get you drunk."

"True, but it does keep you from having a hell of a hangover."

I look him up and down, and even though I'm well past tipsy, I can see that he's hot. Like…smoking hot. Set off the fire alarms all by himself hot. The suit he's wearing doesn't disguise the fact that he's ripped, and his face has got all those angles that they talk about when they say 'classic beauty.' I'd be just fine in the morning if I could stare at him all night.

He's laughing now, a rich baritone that tells me I spoke out loud without even meaning to. "If you're going to stare at me all night, then you're going to drink some water. Don't move; I'll get some."

I roll my eyes as he turns his back and I down the rest of my drink. Hot and a party-pooper. I think I'll have a better time on the dance floor. Before I know it, I'm in the middle of the writhing bodies, losing myself in the music. I don't need a man tonight—even if he is sexy as fuck. I don't know why I felt bad earlier. Nothing can be bad when you feel this good. I love dancing. I don't know why I don't go dancing more.

Hands land on my hips and I spin to find

the sexy man on the dance floor with me. He's a really good dancer, and he guides us with a quiet confidence that only turns me on more. I don't mind the way his hands are wandering further than I would normally let them. I want them to wander. I want him to make me feel good.

I press my back against his chest and his arm slips around my waist, pinning me against him as our hips move together. He's hard against my back and it makes my heart race. I can't remember the last time someone was so obviously turned on by me. It's hot and it makes me want more—to push him so he can't help but sweep me off my feet and carry me away. I push my ass back into him, and suddenly his lips are on my neck, and damn, I can feel those lips *everywhere*. It's a good thing I wore underwear because I'm clearly not in control of myself, and Lily's wedding is the last place I want to make a fool of myself.

Mr. Sexy's hand dips lower, teasing me with brushing fingers through the fabric of my dress. If the hem were shorter, I have no doubt that his hand would be underneath it. Arousal surges through me, and I'm shocked by just how much I want that to happen.

Turning to face him again, I find fire in his eyes, and I want that fire in me and all over me. We're not dancing anymore, just standing in the middle of the movement. He weaves his fingers into my hair, tilting my head back just far enough for him to lean down and kiss me, and I know what it means to be lit by that fire. His other arm snakes around my back, holding me against him, and the hand in my hair holds me still while he deepens our kiss. I'm fully wet now, I can feel it, and I try to kiss him back even though I can't really move. He knows what he's doing, and when he pulls away, I'm breathless from more than just the dancing.

Pulling me off the dance floor, we move back to the bar where he hands me the glass of water that he promised to give me earlier. "Drink that."

"And here I thought that you were going to sweep me into a corner and have your way with me."

A sly smile and another raised eyebrow. "We'll get to that, I promise you. But first we're going to deal with the fact that you left when I told you not to move."

I laugh, and it feels good. "I wasn't aware that I needed your permission to dance at my friend's wedding."

His eyes narrow and there's a small frown on his face. "The rules of the wedding were clearly laid out in the invitation. Any unattached subs are to obey any Dom who gives them a command when it's a question of health or safety. I'm concerned about the amount of alcohol you have in your system. So drink the water."

There's an edge to his voice on those last words that has me reaching for the cup, but I stop halfway there. "Wait, what?"

"I don't like having to repeat myself, Emma." His frown is deeper now.

"You think I'm one of those girls that sits at people's feet and does what anyone tells them to do?" I burst out laughing. "Wow, did you misread that one. Look, you're probably one of the sexiest men I've ever had the chance to meet, and damn can you dance. And that kiss—" I stop myself before I can throw myself on him for another one. "But I'm not a sub. I'm not in the 'scene.' I'm not yours to boss around, so you can take your little rules and disappointed frown and *shove them up your ass*."

I realize there's silence in the immediate vicinity, and I see people looking at us. I hadn't realized how loud I was speaking or that I yelled that last part. Even Lily is looking at me and blushing. A wave of embarrassment rolls over me. I'm not usually like this. I don't get this drunk and embarrass my friends at their weddings. Mr. Sexy doesn't look phased, he simply looks at me with a small, infuriating smile.

Unable to look at him or bear the weight of strangers' stares, I grab the glass of water and stalk across the room to an empty table in the corner, as far away from the dance floor as possible. I collapse into the chair and start to drink the damn water, only to find that he's followed me. "What do you want?"

"I'm making sure you drink the water," he says, practically grinning.

"Are you happy about the fact that you just made me embarrass my friend at her wedding?"

"Of course not, but you're cute when you're flustered. And since I already find you beautiful, this is fun to watch."

I glare at him, throwing back the rest of the water like a shot. "Happy?"

"Very."

"Good. You can go away now that you know I'm not a sub. I'm not looking for someone like you."

He tilts his head. "I don't think that's true."

"Wow." I can't help but laugh. "You're very condescending."

"Is it condescending if you're right?"

"You're not."

He pauses for a second, like he's considering something. "Care to let me prove it to you?"

"I'm not having sex with you," I say, rolling my eyes.

"I didn't say anything about sex, but I do

intend to make you come." He takes a step closer, and holds out my hand. "You come with me, and for fifteen minutes, you do exactly as I say. I can show you that you're kidding yourself when you say that you don't need this."

"And this is the part where I go with you and you kill me?" I say sarcastically. But the way he's looking at me, with that fire from the dance floor, has me leaning forward to give him a better view. The idea of an orgasm with this man is infinitely appealing. It's been way too long since I've been given one that was better than my vibrator. A *long* damn time.

"If you're uncomfortable, say 'Red,' and everything stops. It's almost a universally recognized safe word."

"What's your name, anyway?"

He doesn't break the stare. "Matthew Forester."

I stand up, wanting to be closer eye- level even though he still towers over me. Being close to him triggers a sense memory of that kiss, and I feel like I'm being pulled toward him despite standing still. "Tell me why I should do this, Matthew."

"What do you have to lose? Be a submissive for fifteen minutes. Even if I'm wrong—which I'm not—you'll still have an amazing orgasm."

"You're awfully confident," I say, furious at myself for being so breathless.

He leans closer. "I have good reason to be."

We're still for a moment, breathing each other's air, and I'm wracking my brain for any reason why I should say no to this. I'm not coming up with anything, and the way he's smiling tells me that he knows it. "Fine," I say. "Fifteen minutes."

Matthew holds out his hand, inviting me

to give him mine. I do, and he wraps my hand in a firm grip. "Understand that when I say that you're a submissive for the next fifteen minutes, *you are*, Emma. I'm not a Dom who likes hesitation or partial commitment."

I smirk at him. "I'll hold up my end of the bargain if you hold up yours."

"Deal," he says, leading me out of the ballroom.

Chapter 3

The hallways of the hotel are deserted this late at night, but Matthew still leads me down several hallways until we're somewhere dark and even more deserted. I have no idea what makes him pick this spot, but I'm suddenly up against the wall, the solid mass of him pressed up against me in a way that tells me he's just as turned on as when we were dancing.

"Dark hallway," I say, trying to keep my head. "I'm beginning to think you lied about killing me."

He doesn't smile, doesn't rise to my flirting bait, his face is serious and filled with hunger. "I didn't give you permission to speak."

"Excuse me?"

That familiar rage rises up in me and I'm

about to kick him when I see just a hint of a smile on his face. “Fifteen minutes, remember?”

Unfortunately, I do. I press my lips together to keep from snapping at him. I made him a promise. If he doesn’t want me to talk, fine. We’re not here to talk anyway.

“Hands above your head.” His tone doesn’t leave any room for argument, and I raise my hands. Matthew catches them, crossing them at the wrists and holding them captive in one hand. He’s strong—I might as well be wearing handcuffs for all that I’d be able to pull away from him, and my heart beats a little bit faster at the thought. He said to say ‘Red’ if I’m uncomfortable, but I’m not yet, even if my body instinctually recognizes danger.

“If we had more than fifteen minutes,” he says softly, “there are lots of things that I could do to show you what this life is about.

But right now, it's simple. Submission isn't about me holding you down for sex, or about you becoming a doormat. It's about trust, and offering something to one another. At the most basic level, you offer me power over you in exchange for pleasure, and I offer you freedom from having to make every decision."

The most basic level, he said. What are the other levels? But now he's kissing me and I can't think because I'm once again on fire. Hot arousal rolls through me like a wave, and I moan, unable to help myself. Matthew simply chuckles against my lips and deepens the kiss, as if he knew that I would react this way.

I want more of him. *More, more, more* is the chant in my brain, and I try to move, to pull him closer, but I can't. Shock and frustration hit me as I remember that I can't move my arms. He has them pinned against the wall and all I can do is let him kiss me. My breath goes short in my chest, and I realize that he's made me wet again. Damn him for being such a good kisser, because that's all it is. I'm turned on from the kiss, and not from the fact that he's restricting my movement.

He pulls away for a moment. "Spread your legs."

I do.

"Farther."

I do, and I'm wobbly on my feet, unstable. If he let go of my arms, I'd probably fall. Which, it dawns on me, is probably the point. His lips brush my ear. "I'm going to touch you now, Emma. I'm going to give you pleasure." Looking me in the eye, his face goes serious again. "And you do not have permission to come."

"What?" The word flies from my mouth before I even realize it.

"You may not come until I allow it. End of discussion. And if you speak again, you won't be permitted to come at all."

I don't doubt it. I bite down on my lip to keep the words inside my head. Regardless of what he's making me do, I need to come. I've been too turned on and I think if I had to stop, I might start crying. You never want me to start crying when I'm drunk—I'll never stop.

Matthew's free hand trails up my leg, bringing my skirt with it until he reaches my panties and brushes them aside. He tries to hide it, but there's a short burst of air from him when touches me. "You're wet for me, and all I've done is kiss you. And restrain you," he grins.

I'm dying to say something, to find a witty comeback, but I keep my lips closed because his fingers are right there, so close to where I want them. His thumb smooths circles around my clit and I gasp because god, that feels good, and it's been a long time since anyone has touched me. That sweet pleasure is sizzling under my skin and we've barely started. I'm guessing we still have ten minutes left, and I'll probably spontaneously combust before that.

One finger—just one—slides inside me and my body arches away from the wall into him, a reflex I can't control. God, why is this so amazing? He's moving slowly, pushing in and out of me, taking his time. His finger curls, stroking that elusive spot just inside that makes my whole body shake. I can feel the beginnings of an orgasm coming together already, and now I know why he has good reason to be confident.

Another finger now, and Matthew is moving faster. I squirm between him and the wall, trying to move closer, do anything that will get me off faster, but between his hands and the way he has me pinned, I'm entirely at his mercy. I close my eyes, sinking into an unfamiliar sensation of blankness. The only thing that is left is the feeling of his fingers teasing me, sending spikes of pleasure through me.

He takes me up and up and up until I'm gasping with need. I'm trying to force my hips down onto his hand faster because I'm so close. Never have I been this desperate to come. I want it—need it—now.

Matthew is watching my face, and I blush because I don't know that I've ever been watched so closely during sex. Or maybe ever. "You're close," he says. It's not a question.

I nod because I don't think I'd be able to speak; even if he gave me permission.

"Good." And then he stops. Just freezes with his fingers still inside me, and my building orgasm trips and falls over into nothing. I groan because being that close and losing it makes me ache. I want to ask him why he would do that, but I also want him to fuck me with his hand again, and if I ask him why, I don't think he will.

"You would have come," he says simply, as if he can read the questions racing across my brain. "And I'm not ready for that." Glancing down at his watch he says, "We still have five minutes together."

This guy isn't a Dom, he's a sadist, and I'm calling him all kinds of names in my head that would probably piss him off. He smiles, easing his fingers back into motion and adding another one. That extra finger fills me up and my breath goes short because it feels impossibly, improbably better than before. Matthew captures my mouth with his, mimicking the motion of his fingers with his tongue, and I'm ready to come apart again. I moan against his mouth, but he doesn't relent.

I'm not sure how I'm supposed to hold back an orgasm like this—it's rising and overwhelming and oh my god I'm so close. Matthew pulls his face back abruptly, never missing a beat with those clever fingers. "I want you to count backwards from thirty," he says. "Out loud. And when you reach one, you have permission to come. Not before."

My mouth falls open. He can't be serious, can he? I won't make it that long. I can't. It's not possible.

"The faster you count, the faster you get to come."

Numbers start to fall out of my mouth faster than I thought I could speak. "Thirty, twenty-nine, twenty-eight…"

And of course he doesn't go easy on me, he speeds up, fucking me with his fingers so fast that I think I'm going to go blind with the pleasure. Every thrust pushes against my G-spot and my voice is desperate, pleading.

"Fifteen, fourteen, thirteen, twelve…"

Oh god oh god oh god I'm not sure how he can even understand the rest of the numbers, they're more moans than words and I'm starting to crack, the pleasure leaking out, pulling me in as he holds me right at the edge, and then "fivefourthreetwoONE!" and everything explodes. I come, the orgasm ripping through me like a storm and leaving me spent and heaving against the wall, still pinned and spread open while the pleasure has its way with me. Matthew's thumb brushes my clit, and I come again. The orgasm wracking my body so hard that if he let me go, I wouldn't be standing.

Sharp, high notes of pleasure spiral through my stomach and up and out until it's enveloping all of me, and I know that I've never had an orgasm like that before.

I come back to the world out of breath, noticing that it's the only sound in the hallway. Matthew's fingers are still inside me, unmoving, his hand like iron around my wrists. "I think time's up," he says, a wicked grin on his face. Gently, he removes his hand, casually bringing it to his mouth. I can see how his fingers are slick with my wetness, and the sound he makes while he tastes me has me wet all over again. "I wish we had more time," he says, "I have so much more that I'd like to do. But," he releases my hands and helps me back to a normal standing position, "a deal is a deal."

There's a small part of me that wants to ask for more, to say that we can have more time. But I know that if I say that he'll ask for more from me. He'll want me to obey him and pretend I'm a submissive little thing like those women at the reception, and I'm not. I am not.

Instead, we walk side-by-side back to the ballroom.

"So you got me to pretend to be a part of your world for fifteen minutes. What was the point?"

He looks over at me as we walk, and I can practically hear him thinking, deciding what to say. "Do you need there to be a point?"

"No, I don't. But that doesn't mean that you weren't trying to make one."

Matthew laughs, a brilliant sound that rings down the empty hall like sunshine. "You're not wrong."

"Are you going to tell me what it is?"

"If you think you can handle it."

I roll my eyes. "What, you think that taking me and giving me an orgasm in a less-than-conventional way is going to change my mind and make me rethink who I am?"

He stops at the door to the ballroom, and the music spills out, partially covering his words and making it feel even more intimate as I lean in to hear him. "I've been a Dom a long time," he says, "and I'm very good at it. When you're a Dom, you practice reading people. You have to because noticing people's cues, the smallest reactions, can make the difference between a scene being amazing or a disaster."

"And if that doesn't work, I'm sure you can just tell the woman how to feel and she'll say, 'yes, sir.'"

Matthew frowns, but he doesn't reprimand me. "Because I've gotten so good at reading people, I can tell very quickly if someone is submissive. That includes whether or not *they* know they're submissive."

"I'm not," I say, ignoring the pointed

look he's giving me and walking into the ballroom. I see Lily not far from the door, and her eyes are on both me and Matthew.

He calls out after me, "How would you know?"

"I thought that little experiment was trying to prove that. I didn't walk out of that hallway begging you to take me, begging you to dominate me. That's not what I want or need."

He's silent for a long moment, and then he walks towards me slowly, his gaze never leaving mine. "I'll make a bet with you."

I snort. "The last time I gambled on my sex life I lost pretty badly, so no thanks."

"You stay with me for three days. You be a submissive—my submissive—for three days, and I'll prove to you that I'm right." He continues on like I never spoke and I'm struggling not to roll my eyes.

"Do you always have to be right?"

"No," he says, closing the remaining gap between us, "I don't. But you *are* submissive."

"I'm not."

"Prove it."

We stare at each other in silence for a moment before he breaks it. "Come stay with me, and if you're right, if you're not submissive and you have no desire to continue in this lifestyle, you'll never have to see me again."

I scoff, "So you get to have me as your plaything for three days and then you just disappear? That doesn't sound like it's much of a bet. What's in it for me?"

Matthew tilts his head, thinking. "If you win–if you aren't in fact a submissive, then I'll give you $100,000 for your trouble." I open my mouth but nothing comes out, and he continues, "But if I win, which I will, and you beg me to keep dominating you, you'll stay with me for another thirty days. And I'll get to show you *exactly* how submissive you are." His voice drops to a whisper on those last words, so low that it's like a caress down my spine, and I shiver.

The orgasm and this conversation have sobered me up, and I honestly don't think I'm so drunk that I'm not thinking clearly, but I don't see a downside. I'm not submissive, there's no way that I can lose this bet. It's like agreeing to have some great sex and then getting a cash bonus. "All right," I say. "You're on."

I hold out my hand and he shakes it, the look on his face nothing but smug. "I look forward to it." And just like that he turns and walks away, disappearing out the same door we just came through.

Suddenly a hand falls hard on my shoulder, spinning me around. "Are you out of your mind?" It's Lily, her eyes wide with disbelief. “Did you really just make that bet?”

“Of course I did. I’m not into this, Lil. There’s no way I can lose.”

She doesn’t look convinced. “Are you sure? Matthew is a good guy, and he’s an incredible Dom, but he can be intense.”

“Yeah, I noticed,” I say, laughing.

She shakes her head. “When he asked me what your name was I didn’t know that this was his plan.”

I pull Lily over to a nearby table where we can both sit. “I don’t think it was. He assumed I was a sub and that’s why I went off on him. I’m really sorry that I embarrassed you.”

“Oh, don’t worry about that. I wasn’t embarrassed, just concerned. The last thing I wanted was for something bad to happen to someone at the wedding.”

I’m laughing again, still a little bit drunk,

"Trust me, there was nothing bad about what just happened."

Lily giggles, and then she sighs. "I miss this. I miss you. How did we let it go so long?"

"I don't know, but we really need to get better at it. When you get back from your honeymoon, we'll make some plans and actually stick to them."

"That sounds perfect."

I pull her into an awkward chair hug. "I hope you know that I really am happy for you. And I hope you get to have lots of kinky sex on your honeymoon."

"Oh, don't worry," she says, giving me a conspiratorial look, "I know that Mark has lots of plans. And speaking of the honeymoon, we're about to make our exit."

People are gathering at the other end of the ballroom toward the exit, ready to wave goodbye to the happy couple as they take off for their honeymoon in Bali. “Let’s go send you off then!”

“Are you sure you’ll be all right?” she asks.

“You said he was a good guy, right?”

Lily nods quickly. “He is. Mark is one of his good friends, and I’ve never seen him do anything that would make me think less of him. Every sub I’ve met that’s been with him has said that he’s wonderful.”

“In that case, I’m sure that I’ll be fine.” I loop my arm through hers. “Now let’s get you off on so you can stop worrying about *my* sex life and focus on your own.”

She grins, and we walk to the other side of the ballroom where Mark is waiting for her. He takes her arm and I watch as they exit the building surrounded by sparklers and confetti. Before they get in the car, Mark dips her back in a heated kiss that makes my chest ache. I’m happy that she’s happy, and I can only hope that someday I'll have that. And that I'll find it on my own terms and no one else's.

Chapter 4

Morning comes way too early, and with it comes a pounding headache. If Matthew were here, I'm sure that he would say that he told me so.

I roll over in the hotel bed and glance at the clock. Nine. I've got plenty of time, but I want to get on the road home. It's a couple of hours away and it would be nice to spend part of the weekend relaxing instead of arriving home and going straight to bed for work on Monday.

Dragging myself out from under the covers, I head to the bathroom. There's a letter on the floor in front of my door like someone slipped it underneath. No idea what that is. I use the bathroom first, and pick up the letter on the way back to spend a few more minutes in bed. But I stop when I see my name on the envelope. The handwriting is neat and efficient and I can think of only one person who would have a letter delivered to my room.

I'm not even going to question how he got my room number. He was clever enough to get my name from Lily before I even spoke to him, I'm sure he's charming enough to have a letter delivered to my room. I tear it open and the page is filled with the same neat handwriting, the black ink stark and almost harsh in the morning light.

Through my hungover haze, I realize I'm just staring at the words and not actually reading. I need to focus.

Emma, I hope you got a good night's rest.

He then outlines the terms of the bet we

made last night. I will spend three days with him as his submissive, and if I win and want to walk away, I get one hundred grand. If he wins, he gets me for another month.

I understand that you had a lot to drink, and if you're no longer willing to make this bet, I would understand. However, if you're still willing, text me your address and I'll have a car pick you up on Friday at eight A.M. You won't need to bring anything with you.

Hoping to hear from you,

Matthew Forester

His phone number is written below his signature, and suddenly I have anxiety that I didn't feel last night in the middle of my buzz and the afterglow of the best orgasm that I've ever had. Three days alone with him where I have to obey him? Now, in the light of day, I'm not sure I can handle that.

But you know what? He didn't say that I had to text him today, and if he doesn't even want to send the car until Friday, I have some time to think, and even with Lily's endorsement, you can be sure that I'm going to Google the hell out of this guy when I get back to my apartment. I put the letter in my bag and take a shower, gather my things and grab breakfast downstairs before checking out. In that amount of time I manage to avoid obsessing over the elephant in the room. Actually, the elephant in my brain. But as I'm heading to my car, I can't take it anymore. I text my friend Jess, who is probably my best friend since Lily and I drifted apart.

Need a vent and advice session. Meet

me at my place when I'm back?

She responds right away.

How long till you're there?

I tell her my ETA and she agrees to meet me and to bring the nachos. Now all I need to do is make it two hours alone in the car without thoughts of Matthew circling endlessly in my mind. Yeah, right.

***

I try everything, but the entire ride back I'm thinking about our fifteen minutes, and by the time I get back to my apartment on the outskirts of Atlanta, I'm so turned on I'm wondering if I shouldn't have invited Jess over after all. But her car is already outside my building, and she's going to be expecting some major gossip, so that ship has sailed and disappeared over the horizon.

Jess opens the door as I arrive—she must have heard me struggling with my suitcase coming up the stairs. Only two nights away from home and I swear, I packed my entire life. That's one nice thing about Matthew's plan; I don't have to bring *anything*. Which is both terrifying and kind of relieving. I hate packing and I consider it one of the banes of my existence, along button-gaps on shirts and the fact that donuts have calories.

"So," she says when I'm barely through the door, "what's going on?"

"Wine first, talk second."

She points to my coffee table. "It's already poured."

"Geeze, woman," I laugh. "You really want to know what happened."

"That and I was bored. Andrew is out of town this weekend and I was reduced to starting *Grey's Anatomy* over from the beginning." She shoves some nachos in her mouth so I can barely understand her. "This seemed more interesting."

I kick off my shoes and flop onto my favorite chair, not bothering to move my suitcase from by the door. That can wait. "So, the wedding was… interesting."

"How so?"

I take a bite of the nachos and relish the crappy cheese and salsa. Nothing makes you feel better after a hangover and a long drive than junk food. "It turns out that my friend, Lily, lives the BDSM lifestyle and I had *no* idea."

Jess's jaw drops open, and she stares. "Oh my god, that's why the thing on the invitation said it would be non-traditional."

I snort. "Yeah, you could say that. More than half the people there were into it, too. There was a couple at my table—who were really nice and shockingly normal—but she sat at his feet the whole time."

"No. Fucking. Way! Dude, that's wild. You don't really think about people who do that getting married or going to weddings, but they're still people. I feel like my mind has been blown."

I laugh and scoop a bigger bite of nachos off the plate. "Let me assure that it hasn't. Not yet."

Jess curls her feet up on the couch and pulls her wine glass closer. "Tell me more."

Taking a sip from my own glass, I tell her everything that happened. *Everything*. Her face gets more and more incredulous as I speak, and when I tell her about the letter at the hotel this morning, she doesn't believe me until I retrieve it from my bag.

"Oh my god," she says. "Oh, my god. Oh. My. God."

I finish my wine. "I'm pretty sure you've

exhausted every intonation of that sentiment."

"What are you going to do?"

"I honestly have no idea." I cover my face with my hands. "That's why I texted you."

She shakes her head. "My mind is definitely blown now."

"Thought it might be."

We're quiet for a second, both of us thinking. "What do you know about him?"

I shrug. "Lily says he's a good guy, but other than his name and the fact that he can give one hell of an orgasm, nothing."

"This calls for research. Where's your laptop?"

"Bedroom desk."

She goes and grabs it, probably because she senses that I've turned into a human slug determined not to move for the rest of the night. "Okay, what's his name?"

"Matthew Forester."

"Matthew Forester," she says quietly as she types. "OH MY GOT HE'S HOT!"

"I KNOW!"

She looks at me. "Emma, girl, you were holding back. The guy that you described did not look like a fucking Greek god in my head. This man should be made into statues. Preferably naked statues. You had his fingers *inside* you, and you hold back on just how attractive he is? Hell, I say you go just so that you can actually say you slept with someone that hot."

I started laughing halfway through her tirade and now I can't stop. "I promise next time I'll try to paint a better picture of the hotness."

"You fucking better."

"Is there anything about him other than the fact that he's been blessed by the beauty fairy?"

She squints at the screen. “Yep. He actually has his own Wikipedia page, so you’ve got a lot of info. Looks like he owns a giant pet food company.”

“Pet food?”

Jess giggles. “Not exactly sexy, but it also says that he has a huge property and that he rescues animals from slaughter houses and kill shelters. Especially exotic ones that people can’t adopt. He helps them get placed in zoos or special homes. Okay, that’s sexy.”

“Let me see?”

She passes me the laptop, and there he is. There’s a professional picture of him in a suit and it looks *damn* good on him. There’s basic biographical information—he’s thirty-three. Four years older than me is not a bad age difference. I thought he might be older than that, but I suppose the ‘Dom’ thing makes people more serious and seem a little older.

"These pages usually have some information about the person's personal life. They don't have anything for him past high school."

Jess frowns. "Huh. Yeah, that's weird. But some people are really private. Especially rich people. And if he's into what you say, I would do everything in my power to keep that off the web. I mean, there's nothing wrong with it, but I can see it being awkward if it came up during like…a business deal or something."

"That's true…"

I feel like I'm being pulled in two different directions. On one hand—the normal and rational hand—it's crazy to stay for three days at a house with a man who I don't know. Like, that's insane. But on the other hand, you get a feeling for someone when you're with them, especially when you're doing what we did. And even though he was playing the part of a Dom, I never felt unsafe. Plus, Lily vouched for him.

A little voice speaks in my head, that maybe it was the alcohol that made her recommendation sound so glowing. I hate to text her on her honeymoon, but she won't be back by the time I have to make my decision. I pull out my phone, and Jess sees.

"You're texting him?"

"Not yet," I say. "I'm texting Lily again, just to make sure that he really is a good guy and it wasn't my tipsy brain interpreting it wrong."

"Good call."

I send off the text, but there are nerves still churning in my gut.

"Honestly, I'd do it, Emma."

"But you see how crazy this is, right?"

She shrugs. "So? I don't know any girl who hasn't had a fantasy about being tied up from time to time, and with a man that hot, I think any woman would say 'yes, please.' Besides, you're not into this stuff like he is, so take the win. Go, have some amazing sex, and get paid for it."

I laugh. "When you put it that way, it sounds like I'm a prostitute."

"Who cares? Three days of sex with a millionaire at a mansion plus money? If you decline, find out if he'll take me instead."

Wine almost comes out of my nose because I'm laughing so hard. "I'll do that."

My phone chimes, and I see that it's Lily.

No, you weren't so drunk that you misinterpreted. Matthew is a stand-up guy. I swear he's not crazy, and you'll be perfectly safe if you go. I think you might be in a little over your head with him, but you don't have to worry about his sanity.

I read the text aloud, and Jess frowns. "What does she mean by that."

"He can be really intense," I say. "If I go, it's not going to be some kind of game where I pretend to do these things, he'll actually expect me to do them."

"Ah. Okay. Well I still say that I'd do it, but you don't have to decide right now."

I nod. "I think I'm going to sleep on it and see what I think tomorrow. Maybe Tuesday."

"You'll tell me if you decide to go, right?"

"Of course," I laugh. "I'm counting on you to be the one who notices if I disappear."

She laughs and finishes her wine. "You got it. Don't think about it too hard, okay? It's a big decision, but whatever you decide is okay. There isn't a right answer."

"Thanks, Jess."

She grabs her bag and waves on the way out the door. “See ya, *submissive*.”

I throw a pillow at her but she closes the door and it hits with a soft *thump*. I hear her laughter as she walks down the hallway.

It was good to talk it out with her, but I still have no idea what I want to do. How do I possibly make this decision?

Chapter 5

I make it all the way through Monday without texting Matthew. I've looked at his letter so many times that it's starting to get worn, and I have his number memorized. I keep going back and forth between wanting the fun and the escape, and telling myself that it's not worth the risk. Then I think of how much that money would help me, and I'm back to thinking about going.

Luckily I don't have any big clients right now, so my bosses don't notice that I'm almost terminally distracted. It's the middle of the summer, and it's a relatively slow time for our public relations firm. All the events taking place now were planned months ago, and there are far fewer companies that want a big push for fall. This is Georgia, after all. So instead of keeping busy, my mind is running the same damn loop over and over.

On top of that, I can still remember the feel of his hands on me, and the cadence of his voice when he promised what he would show me if I lost the bet. If I take it, I have no intention of losing, but that utter confidence is still alluring. Intriguing. If he weren't so damn determined to prove that I'm one of his little submissive girls, then I would have already said yes. But then again, if he wasn't into it, I would never have met him in the first place.

This entire situation has way, way too many angles in it. I can barely wrap my head around it. That's what keeps my hands off my phone for all of Monday, and most of Tuesday. It's Tuesday evening when everything snaps into clear focus. This isn't an opportunity I'll ever get again. Who cares if he's trying to make me submissive? I know that I'm not, so why wouldn't I just say yes? If I have nothing to lose, why would I say no? I was having some lingering guilt about making him feel bad by winning, and that's bullshit. He offered, and if he's willing, then so am I. Hell, I could use a little sex-filled getaway. Our little interlude is the most sex I've had in over a year, and now that I remember what it's like, I want more.

I grab my phone and enter the number, writing about seven different versions of my message before I actually hit send.

I accept the challenge. Get your checkbook ready.

I send that, quickly followed by my address.

Not even ten minutes later my phone chimes.

I was beginning to think you had forgotten about me.

You pinned me to a wall and fucked me, I think that's a little hard to forget.

Good. I was hoping you'd be thinking about it. And me.

Damn it, I walked right into that one. He was checking to see what kind of impression he made. I had decided to play it cool, but that's out the window if he knows that I can't stop thinking about that night. I try to think of the perfect response, but it's easier to be witty face-to-face.

Don't worry, I'm only doing this for the money.

I can almost feel him laughing on the other side of the phone.

I thought you might say that. I'll make you forget all about the money.

You can try.

Oh, I will.

The little texting bubbles appear for longer than before, and I'm on the edge of my seat, waiting to see what he might say. Is he going to give me instructions for Friday? But when the text actually comes through, my jaw drops.

When you're spread open underneath me, coming over and over again on my mouth and cock, money will be the last thing on your mind. What do you say to that?

It takes me a second to breathe, imagining the scenario he painted, my body conjuring up sense memory of him to complete the scene. Dammit, now I'm wet and flushed and this isn't how I thought the conversation was going to go. He's better at this game than I am, and I need to step back and think about that. I need to be ready so that when I'm face to face with him, I don't get blindsided by the sheer force of his charm and will.

So you Doms don't mince your words, do you?

I don't. And for the record, the only acceptable response to the above, is 'Yes, Sir.'

Go to hell.

Get it out now. When you're here, your ass will be under my hand for speaking to me that way. And believe me, that will be more fun for me than it is for you.

There's a small winking face at the end of that text, mocking me. I have no words for what's going on in my body and brain right now. Then another text.

Sweet dreams, Emma.

Sweet dreams? With the way I'm feeling, my dreams are going to be anything *but* sweet. Hot, sweaty, and unfulfilling is more like it. I don't text him back—I'm too busy digging through my dresser drawer to find my under-used vibrator. I'm not even *there* yet and he's got me so tuned up that I have to get off. What have I gotten myself into?

Chapter 6

Matthew continues to text me on Wednesday and Thursday, and even though I'm not a prude, the blatant sexuality of his texts still makes me blush. My vibrator has gotten more use in the last two days than in the last six months combined, and it feels like it's not enough. Suddenly there's a sex-starved monster inside me and she will stop at nothing until she's fed.

There's mention of how he's going to taste me. How he's going to take me slowly. How he's going to make me beg. I threw that last one back in his face, but he just laughed. I don't know what it is about his utter confidence that fascinates me. If it were someone else I think it would drive me up the fucking wall, but with him it somehow works. I know I barley know him, but somehow I can't imagine a Matthew that wasn't that confident.

Thursday night, I text him.

Are you sure I don't need to bring anything? Not even a toothbrush?

He texts back instantly, like he was waiting for it.

No. Everything is taken care of.

Okay. That's nice. I don't remember a time that a trip was stress-free like this. It's not even that long of a trip. Yesterday he told me where he lives, and it's on the other side of Atlanta. A little far from the city, but not so far into the country that I'd consider it isolated. I've scoured the internet for pictures of his house, but there are none. There are barely any pictures of the animal sanctuary that he's famous for.

I haven't gotten up the nerve to ask him why there's nothing about him online. Somehow I figure that's a better in-person question.

Typically, right before I take off for a weekend, I'm packing frantically. I don't really know what to do with myself since I'm not. When I texted Jess earlier to tell her that I was going, she suggested that we get drunk and celebrate, but I really don't want to show up at his house hung over, so I said no. Lily just texted me a smiling face. I know she'll want to hear as many juicy details as Jess when I come back, and when she gets back from her honeymoon.

Eventually, I settle on reading. I've had books on my nightstand for ages that I've been meaning to pick up but somehow I never find the time. I read until my eyes won't stay open anymore, and I force them open just long enough for me to set my alarm. There's no turning back now.

***

A limousine. He sent me a fucking limousine. This isn't what I thought he meant when he said that he'd send a car, but the giant, black, shining monstrosity is stretched out in front of my apartment building and there's even a uniformed driver waiting by the door.

"Ms. Silverman?" he asks as I walk up.

"That's me," I say, and allow him to open the door for me. I slide into the limo and realize that I've never been in one before. I've never had 'let's rent a limo' type friends. It always seemed like an unnecessary extravagance. Now that I'm inside one, I think we may have miscalculated. This is *fantastic*. There are little water bottles and so many air vents I could probably have the air conditioning blowing on every part of my body at once.

I lie down on one of the bench seats as we begin to move. How often do you get to lounge in a limo alone? I might as well take advantage of it. But almost immediately I'm cold and have to turn the air conditioning down. I had no idea what to wear today—what do you wear to meet the man who's going to boss you around for three days? —and I ended up in a halter top and jeans. Too much exposed skin on my top half to have the air blasting.

With it on a lower setting, it's way more comfortable, and I start to drift off. I woke up multiple times this morning afraid that I had missed my alarm, and I'm sleepy. I don't even notice I'm drifting off, but a jolt under the wheels wakes me, and I see that the city is gone and we're driving down a lane with tall trees on either side. Through the foliage, a house appears, and I have a hard time keeping my jaw off the floor. That's not a house, that's a fucking mansion.

All old stone and ivy with one of those circular driveways that every rich person seems to have, it's easily one of the most beautiful houses I've ever seen. I can't even imagine what the inside looks like. We pull up to the front doors—double and glass covered in wrought iron—and Matthew steps out of them, coming down to greet me.

He's wearing jeans too, which makes me feel better, and a button down with the sleeves rolled to the elbows. I know plenty of women who would write songs about those forearms, and I'm determined to make sure that he never knows that I'm one of them. He stands on the bottom of the wide stone steps leading up to the door and waits.

The chauffeur hurries around and opens

the door. “Thank you,” I say, realizing that I could easily have opened the door myself if I hadn’t been ogling Matthew and the house.

“No problem, Miss. Enjoy your day.”

Now that I’m face-to-face with Matthew, I have no idea what to say. He’s still sexy as fuck, and after all our racy text messages, I’d be happy to skip directly to the fucking. I don’t think that’s going to happen, though. We both stand silent as the limo disappears down the drive, and until there’s nothing but the sound of birds to hear.

“Good morning,” he says, smiling a little.

“Morning.”

“How was the drive?”

I stretch my arms and back. “I slept for most of it. The car was really comfortable. I’d never been in a limo before today, I didn’t expect it to rock me to sleep.”

Matthew chuckles. “I’m glad you liked it. Come on, I have breakfast waiting. I thought we'd talk for a bit."

"Talk?" I raise an eyebrow, "We're not going straight to the dungeon?"

He doesn't miss a beat. "You'll be happy to know that my playroom has heat and carpeting. I'd hardly call it a dungeon. But no, we're not going directly there."

I follow him into the house and a gorgeous entryway decorated in shades of cream. It looks like one of those houses you see in films, perfectly staged with a blend of art and antiques. "This is beautiful."

"Thank you," he smiles over his shoulder at me. "I'll give you the grand tour after breakfast."

"From how big it looks on the outside, the grand tour might take the whole three days."

"It does seem that way sometimes," he says, chuckling again.

This is definitely not what I expected. I

mean, I knew he was rich and that he'd live someplace big and gorgeous, but I was expecting something more…gothic. This is the opposite. It's light and open and doesn't feel the least bit oppressive. I suppose it's not fair that I would assume that, but still… even lily's wedding was black and crimson. Even though it's extravagant, it's shockingly normal. Peaceful, even.

We're winding our way through hallways that are smaller than I imagined, and suddenly we're at a tiny door and back out into sunlight. A small courtyard of brick and ivy is on the other side, with a bistro table and chairs. Breakfast is laid out on the table; everything from croissants and orange juice to what I think might be apple strudel.

"One of the house's little secrets, and my favorite breakfast spot," he says as he sits.

I take the seat opposite him. This doesn't seem real. It's like a movie or something.

"So what are we talking about?"

"Well," he says, an amused look on his face, "I thought we could get to know each other a little better before we talk about how things will go for the next few days and negotiate."

"Negotiate?" I wasn't aware I was going to have to haggle.

"We'll get to that. Tell me a little bit about yourself, and feel free to eat."

I grab a croissant off one of the plates in front of me and move the butter over so I can reach it. "To be honest, there's not a lot to tell about me. I live on the other side of Atlanta, and I work as a Junior Publicist at Jones & Burke."

"That's an excellent firm."

I nod. "I majored in marketing in college and got an internship there. I was lucky enough that they wanted to hire me right after I graduated. I've been there ever since.

I don't have any roommates or pets. A few close friends. My parents have both passed away."

"How do you know Lily?"

"We were roommates in college," I say around the bite of croissant I just shoved in my mouth. "She was my best friend. We're both terrible at keeping in touch and we live just far enough apart that it's inconvenient to see each other. The wedding was the first time I'd seen her in person for two years."

He looks surprised at that. "So when you came to the wedding, did you know that she was in the lifestyle?"

"I had no idea. My invitation said that the wedding would be non-traditional and that's it."

He laughs that same ringing laugh that I remember from that night, and my breath catches. It really is a beautiful laugh. "You must have been shocked."

"That's one word for it."

"Well, I'm sure that's not all that I need to know about you, but those are good basics. What would you like to know about me?"

I take another bite of croissant—which is absolutely perfect—and swallow before I answer. "I Googled you."

There's that half-smile again. "So you already know the basics."

"Kind of, though I couldn't find any pictures of this place on the internet."

Matthew nods. "I prefer to keep my private life private. I'm not enough of a celebrity to have to worry about press or paparazzi out here, but when you live my lifestyle, keeping a low profile is important. As I know you're aware, not everyone is comfortable with kink, and I want everyone in the scene who visits my home to feel safe."

"That's a good reason."

He raises an eyebrow. "Were you thinking of bad ones?"

"Maybe."

He shrugs. "I suppose from an outside point of view it does seem odd."

I finish my croissant and pour myself a glass of juice. "So what are we negotiating?"

"You certainly cut to the chase."

I try my best not to glare at him. "I want to know what I'm getting myself into."

"Very well," he clears his throat. "I've gone back and forth on what I should expect from you. Every Dom/sub relationship is different, and every aspect is negotiated so both parties are comfortable. Since you're new to the lifestyle, I'm willing to bend a little more toward vanilla. Or what you'd call 'normal.'"

"Things like what?"

"I don't often have submissives in my

home," he says. "But when I do, I require that they remain naked unless I permit them clothing. I thought that might be a shock for you, so I'm willing to compromise by letting you wear lingerie I have provided."

My mouth falls open, and then I close it again. *You knew what you were walking into, Emma. Remember that. You agreed to come here and do what he said. You're probably going to have sex with him anyway, so lingerie isn't a big deal.* "Fine," I say.

"I also usually require my submissives to address me as 'Sir' or 'Master' at all times. Since we're not in a relationship, you'll only be required to use my title in sexual situations. Keep in mind that I will decide what a sexual situation is and what it is not."

"Your *title*?" I scoff.

A lazy smile crosses his face, and even though he's at ease, I can tell it's not a pleased smile. "Yes, my title. Part of a power exchange is recognizing the person to whom you've given that power. Calling me Sir is a simple way of doing that. Manners and structure are important in BDSM. Have good manners, and you'll be rewarded. Bad manners, and you'll be punished."

I smirk. "Yes, Sir."

"I need you to choose a safeword. You will always be able to use 'red,' but I find it helps for beginners to have more than one."

"How do I pick?"

Matthew reaches forward to the table and pours himself a cup of coffee from one of the pots. "That's up to you. Some people pick something that they hate. Some people pick a word that reminds them of when they feel safest. But it has to be something that you absolutely will not forget, even if you're panicking."

I think about it, and the memory comes

to me almost instantly. Lemon pie on a sunny day and the feeling of utter safety and perfection. "Lemon," I say.

"You won't forget that?"

"Never."

He nods, accepting it. "Good. If you use it, everything stops. Don't use it lightly. It's not something you use if you're unsure or uncomfortable. If you need a moment to check in with me, tell me, or say yellow and we'll slow down."

I nod. I can do that, and it's a relief that we're not going to be hurtling down a path that we can't come back from.

"Moving on. I need to know your boundaries. How far are you willing to go sexually?"

There's a little thrill of surprise that goes up my spine. "I get a choice in that?"

"You get a choice about everything. I'm not going to force you to do anything you're uncomfortable with. It is perfectly possible to have a Dom/sub relationship without sex. In my opinion, sex does add to the experience, but I would never force it."

"I'm fine with sex," I say, feeling a tiny release of tension in my shoulders that I didn't realize was there.

His smile is as bright as the sun that's shining down on us. "I was hoping that you'd say that."

I laugh. "I'm sure you were, based on those text messages."

Across the table I see his eyes darken with heat, and I had forgotten how compelling they are. "I'm very much looking forward to it. But since you said yes, there is something I won't negotiate on: your orgasms belong to me."

I blink at him. "What does that mean? I'm assuming that I'm not going to be having sex with someone else, so of course they belong to you?"

Mathew laughs, and I think that even though he's really laughing *at* me, it's out of delight rather than mocking me. "No, you won't be having sex with someone else. I mean that just like in that hallway, you only come when I allow it. You need permission. You are allowed to ask, and I expect you to tell me if you are so close that you think you can't control yourself, but letting go before I agree will land you in trouble."

"I mean…that's weird, but I guess it's fine."

"I think you'll enjoy it," he says, taking another sip of his coffee. "There's one last thing. You're new to this, and we both know that you're here to prove me wrong. But I still expect you to submit and obey. However, because you're new, I want you to know that at any point if you don't understand a command or you are uncomfortable, I expect you to tell me. Even if I have given you the command not to speak. *Especially* if I've given that command."

"Okay." My voice sounds smaller than I'd like it to.

"Communication is the most important thing between a Dom and a sub, and I don't want you lying to me. You won't hurt my feelings. I need you always to be honest with me, no matter the situation."

I take a sip of my juice. "I can do that."

"Do you have any other questions?"

"Are there…" I swallow, "are there going to be punishments?"

"Possibly."

I wince. "I really don't like pain."

He chuckles, "I'm not a sadist, and I didn't think for a second that you were a masochist. Not all punishments are painful. But," he says, that amused mask back on his face, “if you’re a good girl, you won’t be punished.”

“I’ll do my best.”

He snorts. “I’m sure you will. Come on, I’ll show you the rest of the house and where you’ll be staying.”

I follow him back inside, hoping I didn’t just agree to something I can’t do.

Chapter 7

The house is huge, and every new room seems to be bigger than the last. As Matthew guides me through the house, I'm incredibly aware of him. He guides me with gentle touches to my shoulder and lower back, just enough to sensitize my skin and leave me anticipating when and where he'll touch me next.

On the staircase, there is a window with a view to a pond and a weeping willow. I stopped to appreciate the vista. It looks like it could be a painting. As I turned back to follow him, I found him so close, just looking at me. I thought he was going to kiss me, and even though I was furious with myself for being so into him, for wanting him so badly when it's only been a couple of hours, I wanted him to kiss me with every cell of my being. He was so close that I was shivering, and I know there wasn't a draft.

"You're beautiful, Emma." Three soft words that came from his mouth and had me blushing like I was a teenager. Then he tucked a loose strand of hair behind my ear before taking me by the hand and leading me up the stairs. I don't think I absorbed anything from the tour for the next ten minutes.

Finally, we arrive at what looks like a suite in shades of blue. There's a four-poster bed and a huge window overlooking what must be the back of the property—rolling fields and in the distance what look to be some animals that don't belong there. Is that a tiger? Geeze. Remind me not to go into the backyard at night.

I glance over at the bed and see that a set of lingerie has been laid out. "This is my room?" I ask him.

"It is."

"This is beautiful!"

He laughs again. "I hope you didn't think I was going to keep you chained up in the basement or in a cage or something."

"No." I promise myself it's the only lie that I'll tell him.

"Don't get me wrong," he says mildly, "sleep restraints are fun. But I don't think that's something that you try when you only have three days."

I don't get it. "Why would you restrain someone while they sleep."

"Could be a couple of different reasons," he says, joining me at the window. "Every person in the lifestyle does things a little differently. If it were me, I'd use wrist restraints that attach to the headboard. Of my bed."

"But *why*."

He grins, and I shiver because he looks

like a wolf stalking his prey and it's really fucking hot. "So that I would know that my sub was available for my pleasure any time I chose."

I try to ignore the way my body heats up at the visual of being bound to the bed, ready for sex on his schedule, and I also try to ignore the way that he emphasized '*my* sub' as if he was talking about me. "Oh." It's the only thing that I actually say out loud.

Matthew walks back over to my bed. "I've arranged for a party this afternoon, and I'd like you to wear this." He gestures to the lingerie. "It's a play party—where people in the lifestyle gather and have fun."

"Sex?"

"Yes, sex."

I swallow. I didn't realize that I would be having sex in front of people, and not so soon.

"You will not be having sex at the party,

Emma. It's too soon for that. But you will do whatever else I require of you. The bathroom is stocked with whatever you need for make-up and showering. Please be ready by two o'clock. For now, you do not have permission to roam the house unaccompanied."

Oh, god. "It's starting?"

He nods, and his smile is both kind and sexy at once, an impossible combination that he somehow pulls off. "Yes, it is." He turns to go, and then turns back. "This is your last chance. After this, I will not hold back."

I swallow and nod. "I understand."

He walks out of the room and closes the door, and I am left waiting with the silence inside.

***

It's twelve o'clock when Matthew leaves

me, and even though I know I don't need that long to get ready, I start anyway. I take a long, luxurious shower, enjoying that it's huge and has multiple showerheads pointing at different levels. Halfway through, I realize what those showerheads might be used for and I blush even though I'm alone.

God, the thought of sex in this shower with Matthew opens a whole new door of possibilities in my head, and I end up staying under the water for another twenty minutes just thinking about it. I seriously think about getting myself off, but then I remember that he said I'm not allowed to come. Not even now, when he'll never know?

But he'll know. Somehow he'll look at me and be able to tell and I'll get a first-hand view of what kind of punishments he thinks aren't painful. Guilt eats me up just thinking about doing it. Instead, I quickly get out and dry myself off so I don't have any more temptation.

He didn't lie—there's more than enough make-up and hair supplies in here for ten women. I kind of feel like I'm in a Sephora, complete with the specially-lit mirror that shows more about your face than you ever wanted to know. I dry my hair, and on a whim, I curl it. I don't know if Matthew wants my hair up or down, but I like the idea of having it curled.

The memory of his hand in my hair on the dance floor rises. My hair was curled then too, and I have to say that I wouldn't mind another kiss like that. When my hair is finished, I do my make-up. He didn't leave me any instructions, so I don't do it heavily. I'm not sure what's going to happen today, but what's for sure is that I don't want to end the day looking like a raccoon from either sweat or tears or both.

Finally, the lingerie. It's a corset that's loose enough so I can slip it on, but I'm going to need help tightening it. With it is a little lacy skirt over a thong, the whole set made of a shimmery blue satin that works perfectly with my skin and hair. With a start I realize that he probably had this made specifically for me. No way did he just go pick up something that fit perfectly and suited me so well. I'll have to ask him where he gets custom lingerie for future reference.

By the time I'm ready, I still have a few minutes left, so I explore the room. There's a bookshelf filled with everything from poetry to some erotic novels, a desk filled with pens and stationary, and an armoire that opens to reveal an entertainment center. It's basically like the best hotel room ever. Plus, the view really is beautiful. Most people don't realize Georgia is one of the most beautiful places you could ever go, but it is.

Rolling green hills and huge swaths of land that are untouched. I'm lucky that I didn't have to move from this state to find a job and that I get to stay here.

There's an overstuffed armchair near the window and bookshelf, and I pull down a novel that sounds interesting and read it until two. I lose myself in the first few pages and I don't even hear him approaching until Matthew is opening the door.

He smiles when he sees me curled up in the chair. "You look beautiful."

"You haven't even seen me standing yet."

Standing by the chair, he looks impossibly tall. He's changed as well, darker slacks and a shirt that matches my outfit. "Then stand up and show me," he says, and his tone has that resonant edge that makes me put down the book and stand without hesitation. The corset almost falls down because it's so loose, and I catch it.

"Put your hands on the bedpost and I'll lace you up. You'll need to hold on."

I do, and I feel a little breathless even before he starts pulling on the laces, because the way his eyes are tracking me is sending heat straight through me. I don't remember the last time I was the center of such *focus*. It's…intoxicating.

He begins at the bottom near my waist, fingers brushing skin as he grabs the laces and pulls. It's already tighter than I expected and it's only the first tug. "No wonder women hated these."

Behind me, Matthew chuckles, and his breath tickles my neck. I shiver. "They didn't, actually. The stories about women becoming obsessed with their figures enough to remove ribs are just stories. Corsets were widely regarded as an aid to health and beauty."

"How do you know that?"

"I majored in history in college, and being a Dom, I did research on the subject."

"Oh." My breath is stolen from me as he pulls another string tight.

And another. "If you were to wear this every day, your body would adjust and it wouldn't feel nearly as constrictive. It would seem normal."

"Yeah…" I say, trying to catch my breath. "Normal."

He laces a few more stays in silence, and then, "Did you make yourself come in the shower?"

The question stops me in my tracks. "I wanted to."

"That's not what I asked."

"No."

"No?"

The expectant silence after that word tells me what he wants. "No, Sir."

His lips brush my bare shoulder, sending goosebumps across my skin. “Good girl.”

An unexpected burst of happiness flies up through my chest, the validation that I made the right choice there. He definitely would have known. Or I would have had to lie, which I think would have been worse.

He’s laced more than halfway up my back now, and it’s getting harder to breathe. I tell him that.

“I know.” I bite back the sarcastic retort that’s on my lips, and he chuckles as if he knows I’m on the edge of cursing him out. “I chose a corset today for a reason.”

“You lied and you actually are a sadist?”

“No. I chose it because a corset is an excellent metaphor for a Dom/sub relationship.”

I gasp as he yanks the next string, and he’s right, I do have to hold onto the post. “Oh?”

"You're letting me lace you into this. It's not something you would choose for yourself, but you're submitting to the fact that I want you in this. I'm choosing how tight to lace it, and you're trusting that I won't hurt you by lacing it too tightly. And once you're wearing it," he punctuates his words by pulling it tight, "I may not always be by your side, I may not always be giving you a command, but you'll feel my control. It is a physical reminder of your submission to me."

Those last words are a whisper as his hand slides around the corset and across my stomach. I might as well be naked, the way that hand feels, the heat of it sinking straight through the silk and down to my skin. I'd never thought of a corset like that—of course I hadn't, because I'm not submissive. But he's not wrong.

We finish lacing the corset in heated

silence, and I can't stop thinking about how with every tightening lace he has more control. And for this brief moment, I don't hate it. He finishes. "Walk around the room for a couple of minutes, let your body get used to it."

I walk in circles, trying to take full breaths and unable to. While I'm walking, Matthew goes to a second armoire where I see more lingerie, and he retrieves something out of a drawer. On my next circle he stops me. "Hands, please."

My wrists are out in front of me before I can think, and he's wrapping leather cuffs around my wrists. There's fleece on the inside, and they're more comfortable than I would have thought. "Why these?"

"We'll be in a room full of people, both Doms and subs. These identify you as a submissive." I open my mouth to protest, but he continues. "For today, and in this context, you are. And this," he says stepping behind me and placing a thin black collar around my neck, "makes sure that no one will touch you without my permission."

My heart starts to pound. "You're going to let someone else touch me?"

"I have that right," he says mildly. "But I won't be doing that today, no."

The choker isn't so tight I can't breathe, but it's tight enough that I'm very aware of it. I'm sure that's intentional.

"Can you breathe a little better now?"

I suck in a breath, and I find that I can. "Yes."

"Perfect," he says with a wicked grin. "Time to tighten it more."

Chapter 8

Matthew is merciless with the corset, and yet somehow my body still adjusts as he has me walk around the room. He pulls me over to face the mirror in the armoire door and my breath catches. I look…sexy. I've always had what I thought was a perfectly average body, and the way the corset reshapes it gives me that hourglass look that every girl dreams of having. "Wow."

"Indeed," he says. "Now, the party is already in progress, so we should get downstairs."

"What will I be doing?"

He turns to me. "You don't need to worry about that. I will tell you what is expected of you and when. That's part of being a submissive—trusting your master to make all the decisions in your best interest. And since this is most definitely a sexual situation, you will address me properly for the rest of the afternoon."

I flick my eyes down to the carpet so he doesn't see how having to call him Sir grates on me. And like hell am I ever calling him Master. "Yes, Sir."

He touches me on the head. "Good girl. You may walk behind me."

I'm led through the house, and outside of the bedroom it suddenly occurs to me how ridiculous I must look. Getting dressed up in lingerie in a bedroom is one thing. Parading around a mansion in it is something you only see in music videos. I almost feel like pinching myself, because this can't possibly be real life.

We walk down a hallway that he didn't show me on the house tour earlier, to a thick door that almost looks like a vault. He opens it, and I hear the slight *whoosh* that accompanies soundproof rooms. But that's nothing, because the room in front of me is huge, and full of people having sex. *Kinky* people having sex. I take a step back and find myself pressed against Matthew. His hand lands on my shoulder, erasing any ideas that I could turn and walk the other way.

There are a lot more people than I expected. The room is a big rectangle, and it's filled with equipment I've never seen before. The walls are a warm, nutty brown and there's thick carpet under my feet. Despite the equipment, the room has an air of comfort, especially with the sunlight pouring through big west-facing windows. But the thing that draws my eye the most are the people. Matthew did warn me that this was a party for Doms and subs, and it's so much stranger than I imagined.

I see Jenny and Chris curled into an

armchair together. There's a scream of an orgasm from the far corner, and the sounds of flesh slapping together. I try not to look. You don't watch other people having sex. Matthew guides me over to a small bar where there's a tray of champagne flutes, already full. "You're going to greet our guests. Offer the champagne only to the Doms. I'll be waiting here for you."

He wants me to serve champagne? Seriously? I look at him to see if he'll crack, to see if he's joking, but he only looks at me expectantly. I feel blood rise to my cheeks thinking about what I saw, and what I might have to interrupt. "What if…what if they're busy."

He smiles, amused. "Then you will wait patiently, and watch until they aren't busy anymore."

My blush returns in full force, and I pick up the tray carefully, the glasses tinkling because I'm shaking and nervous and still a bit short of breath from the corset. I glance around the room, and make a decision to go clockwise—better than just picking at random.

The first couple I come across is a man and a woman, the woman completely naked and draped across the man's lap. Her ass is red and I can see very defined handprints on her skin. But she looks, peaceful…almost *blissful* as he strokes her head. What is she feeling that she can be that happy after being hit like that? I extend the tray towards the man. "Champagne?" I can almost hear Matthew clearing his throat behind me. "Sir?"

"Of course," he says, taking a glass. "Thank you."

I move on, ignoring the tenderness I saw on his face as he looked back towards his sub. I serve a woman who's in an armchair, legs perched on the edges while a young man licks into her pussy like it's his last meal. The glazed look in her eyes as she accepts the champagne tells me that he's doing a good job.

There's a woman bound and gagged while her Dom alternately fucks her and drops blows across her skin with a flogger. The sounds she's making don't change—they all sound like she's in the midst of the best sex of her life.

Every couple is like that, and I'm wondering if that's what Matthew wanted me to see. I'm wondering if this is his attempt at making me think that all this is normal. There's another orgasmic scream, and I look up at my next guest, and can't keep my jaw from dropping. I couldn't see before with all the other couples and equipment in the way, but there's a woman strapped to a big wooden X.

She's completely naked, wrists and ankles wrapped in cuffs just like mine, and they're attached to the wood. There's a thump on the floor as her Dom, a man in leather pants and without a shirt, drops the vibrator that he had been using on her. She's writhing against the wood and I can't tell if she's trying to get free or if she's still in the throes of her orgasm. I'm about to offer him some champagne when he unties his pants and lets his cock spring free.

I instinctually look away, and I feel the burning of the flush that's covering what feels like my entire body. I realize I'm looking towards Matthew and he smiles a slow, lazy smiles and nods back towards the couple. He told me that if they were busy I was supposed to wait and watch until they were free. I swallow and look back just in time for him to step up to the X and slip inside her. She moans, and I watch as he begins to fuck her. I watch her face, and even though she doesn't have a choice, she looks okay. She looks more than okay, she looks rapturous.

I imagine myself in her place, and suddenly I can't stop. I think about what it would be like to be in that position, completely vulnerable, and not just anyone, but Matthew the one holding me captive. I'm suddenly wet and aware that the outfit that I'm wearing is not enough to hide it to anyone in the room. The man slams into her, again and again, and I couldn't look away even if I wanted to. It doesn't look she's trapped at all, and seconds later she's begging the man for permission to come. He doesn't give it, and she's writhing on him as he continues to fuck her.

Finally, she asks again and he growls a yes that ends with another orgasmic scream. I don't watch porn often, but if it affects me this much, maybe I should. I'm almost dripping, and I'm tempted to tell Matthew that I'm ready for the sex part of this to start. But I know that it won't happen if I don't stay here and finish the task he's given me.

The man finishes and immediately sets to work unstrapping his sub. She slips limply into his arms and he gathers her in a blanket, settling into a nearby chair. It's not until he glances up towards me that I dare walk forward. He gives me an appreciative glance up and down. "Who do you belong to?"

I grit my teeth, fighting the retort that I belong to no one. But in this context I know the answer he wants, so I lower my eyes. "Matthew."

He reaches out and takes a glass from the tray. "I saw you waiting patiently. I'm sure your master is very proud of you for such excellent service."

I blush again—before today I didn't even

know that I had the capacity to blush this much—and murmur, "Thank you." It feels weird to be complimented for waiting with a tray, but considering how much I wanted to run away, it feels like a victory that someone noticed.

I continue my circuit of the room, and luckily no one else is occupied. When I'm down to one glass on the tray, I approach Jenny and Chris who are at the end of my circuit. But Jenny isn't cuddled in his lap anymore, she's on her knees, and his cock is all the way down her throat. I offer him the tray.

"It's good to see you again, Emma," he says as he takes the final glass. "Though I'm a little surprised. I thought you were on the vanilla side of the wedding."

"I was," I say. "I am. I'm just—"

"Emma and I have a difference of opinion on whether or not she's submissive." Matthew's voice comes from behind me, and a second later I feel the heat of him even though he's not touching me. So close. "I made a bet with her that after three days she would admit it."

I press my lips together, fighting to keep my mouth shut. Chris sees it and laughs. "You're a lucky girl, Emma."

Jenny hasn't as much as looked up from her task while we've talked, and she doesn't give any sign that she's going to.

"If you'll excuse us, Christopher," Matthew says.

"Of course."

Hand on my shoulder, Matthew guides me away, back toward the bar and a secluded corner. I put the tray away and he pulls me into his lap in a chair like the other ones scattered across the room. "You did well," he said.

"I'm guessing you didn't have me do that

because you needed a cocktail waitress."

"You're right," he says, smiling and pulling me closer in his lap. Despite the warmth of the day, I'm getting cold in this outfit, and the heat of his body feels good against mine. I also feel weirdly drained from the experience, and it feels good to just relax. His hand draws circles on my hip, and I let my head rest on his shoulder. "I wanted you to see a bunch of different couples playing, and maybe see some things you'd be curious to try. I also wanted to show you off a little."

"Show me off?"

"You're beautiful," he says, shrugging. "You look sexy as hell in this outfit, and maybe I like to make other people jealous."

I don't say anything. I don't remember a time when someone's wanted people to be jealous of me. It feels…different. All of this feels different than I expected it to.

"Also," he says, "there are different kinds of submissives. Some submissives find great joy in serving others. Some find the most joy in being a submissive all the time, and some are submissive only in the bedroom. Those are generalizations, and there are as many variations as there are people. I wanted to see how serving might affect you." He smiles, and I get distracted by the feeling of his fingers on my skin. "I don't think you are a service submissive."

"Oh." I let myself relax, and even with the sounds and smells of sex around me, I find myself almost drifting off. "What happens now?" I ask through my haze.

"You tell me how you felt while you were watching Karen and Greg."

I blush, and try to push off his lap, but his hands are like iron on me and I'm not able to move. "Who?"

He raises an eyebrow that tells me he

knows I'm only pretending that I don't know who he's talking about. But he's going to let me get away with it. "The couple using the St. Andrew's cross. How did you feel watching them?"

"I didn't feel anything."

"You and I both know that that's not true. There are no secrets between Doms and subs, or at least there shouldn't be. The reason we make rules and talk so much is that the way we play, the stakes are higher. We're not stupid. If one person keeps something from the other, maybe nothing happens. But also maybe one person panics and someone gets hurt. I saw you watching them. Tell me how you felt."

I can't meet his eyes. "I was aroused. They were having sex, that's what happens when you watch people have sex." Closing my eyes, I shake my head. "I still don't understand why she would agree to be tied up like that so that anyone can do what they like with her."

"But you wouldn't agree to do it with just *anyone*," he says gently. "This isn't about signing up to be assaulted by someone you don't know. Anyone who says that doesn't understand BDSM. This lifestyle is all about consent. We call it play for a reason—it's fun. There shouldn't be anything happening that both parties aren't okay with. If you think about it in that context, does it make more sense? It's not really any different than how vanilla people have relationships. Kinky people just prefer more creative sex."

"Maybe," I say, still unsure. I don't say it out loud, but shouldn't it be a sign that something's wrong if you want to be tied up and beaten while you're getting off? I mean, everyone *seems* happy, but is that because they just don't know better?

"So you were aroused," he says. "What

was it that aroused you? Was it just the sex? Or was it the bondage?"

I don't want to admit that it might have been the bondage, but to be perfectly honest, I'm not sure. I didn't start to get wet until he was fucking her, so it could have been either. "I'm not sure."

"Fair enough."

Jenny and Chris are in my line of vision, and he's leaned back in the chair while she sucks him, eyes closed. I'm distracted by the look on her face—a kind of eager joy. Chris reaches out, and when she dives down onto his cock, he holds her head still, rendering her immobile so she has to take his cock deeper. "She can't breathe," I whisper.

"Chris and Jenny have been together a long time. She *is* a service submissive, and she's happiest when she's serving his pleasure. He knows how long she can hold her breath, and he also knows that she trusts him to choose for her whether or not she gets to breathe. She knows that he would never give her something that she couldn't handle, and so she doesn't have to worry or panic about her breath. She'll breathe when he's ready."

"That's so…." A frustrated sound comes out of me. "That doesn't make any sense!"

"Then why are you wet?"

I'd been so relaxed that I hadn't even noticed his hand moving from my hip to my inner thigh and higher to were his fingers are touching me. Where he can feel that I'm embarrassingly wet. It's mortifying, and when I try to move my hands, to push him away, he holds me still. "His pleasure gives her pleasure. And even if it didn't, it's not about the blowjob." Matthews's fingers stroke down my pussy, and I shiver with pleasure. I hate that he's affecting me like this. "Have you ever been able to trust someone like that? So utterly and completely that you'd let them deprive you of air because you know that they'd never hurt you, that they know what you need even better than you do?"

"Nobody can trust anybody that much," I say. "Inside she must be screaming."

He laughs, and it sounds a little sad. "We can ask her when they're finished, if you like." Another stroke across my clit.

"No, thank you." He waits. "Sir."

He laughs softly. "So stubborn. I'm not going to play with you until everyone leaves, but until then, you're going to wait and watch. And with the exception of your safewords and 'Yes, Sir,' you no longer have permission to speak. I think you need some time to think about what you're looking at and how it all fits together."

Again, he waits, and I realize he's waiting for me to agree. "Yes, Sir," I say, though I can't even believe that it's coming out of my mouth.

He lifts me off his lap, and spins me, catching my wrists together, and a tiny click, I can't move my arms in front of me. I can feel the strain on the cuffs and I realize that he's clipped them together. I whirl on him. "What is this?"

His face is not one recognize. It's stern and hard—the face of a Dom. "Sub, I told you not to speak. If you disobey again you will be punished." He's not even looking at me because he's arranging something in my underwear, something small that bumps against my clit. "Now kneel."

I stare at him, glaring, because this isn't what I thought was going to happen. My intent must be pretty clear because he laughs. "I'm your Dom, Emma. I do not have to tell you everything I'm going to do. You agreed to submit, and I'm not crossing any boundaries. You gave me this power over you freely. Now kneel." That last word has so much power in it that I fall to my knees in front of him.

Matthew weaves his fingers into my hair and raises my face so that I'm looking at him. "Good. Now turn to face the room."

I do, and I'm nestled between his legs, hands bound. In this position, it's impossible not to remember what I am here. I had kind of forgotten. I am one of those girls in the room who's just doing what he ways. Why did I agree to this? His hands stroke across my shoulders. "Just look, just watch. Take this time to observe."

Just then the Domme I served comes up to the two of us. "Matthew," she says, her voice like silk. "I thought for a while you weren't going to make an appearance at your own play party."

"I had some things to tend to. But it's

good to see you, Maya." His hands are still on my shoulders.

The Domme looks down on me, and I look at her. Her eyes are a sharp blue, and the way she's looking at me makes me shiver. She's alluring in a way that feels dangerous. "What a lovely little sub you have here."

"This is Emma. She's very new, and I'm introducing her to the lifestyle."

A smile slips across her face like she's had an idea. "If you'd ever like to share, I'd like to see that luscious mouth buried between my legs." My mouth falls open and she laughs. "She is very new, isn't she?"

"Yes. And I'll keep that idea in mind if I decide she needs some female training."

I want to scream that I'm right here, that they can't just talk about me like that, but I can't speak. Matthew told me not to. Besides, I would have no idea what to say to her. I trust that Matthew isn't going to go back on his word and let anyone else touch me today.

Maya walks away. I missed their last words thinking about what I would say if I were allowed to speak. And then the words fly right out of my head, because the little thing in my thong turns on. Oh my god, he put a vibrator on me. Oh god, oh god. I'm still so turned on, that I'm suddenly on edge. Matthew's lips are at my ear. "Time to build some of that trust I was talking about. You do not have permission to move. You do not have permission to speak. You do not have permission to come. You have to trust me. Trust that I'm doing what will bring you the most pleasure. And if you don't trust me like that yet—which I know you don't—remember that I am your Dom, and this is what I want. What do you say?"

I'm leaning back against his legs, the

vibrations flowing through me and I can barely think. I can't breathe. Somehow I find the breath and the words. "Yes, Sir."

"Good girl." He presses a kiss against my neck and it makes the whole thing worse—or better, depending on how you look at it.

The little thing keeps vibrating, pressure building in my spine, and I try to wiggle to relive the pressure. Matthew's hands come down on my shoulders. "I know it's hard. Do. Not. Move."

A sound close to a whimper escapes me, and the heat in my body is making me sweat. I'm not going to be able to hold it back. I can't. I can't. I can't—

The vibrations stop, and I can't help it, I sag with relief. Then Matthew's fingers are in my hair again, twisting my head back so he can take a kiss. Heat surges through me and it's like the vibrator is on as he teases my lips open with his tongue. And then his tongue is tangling with mine and I think I hear a low growl in his throat. When he let's go, I can't breathe for a second. I'm on overload. Can't think.

I heave in a breath and open my eyes to see Jenny and Chris watching me. A couple of others too. A flush rolls across my chest, a tinge of embarrassment with it. But honestly, I'm too full of sensation to care. I was more embarrassed watching than being watched.

"She responds so well to you…" Chris says, chuckling. "Maybe you are right, Matthew. I swear you can smell a sub from a mile away." I glare at him, which only makes him laugh harder. "I don't think she liked that, though. I think everyone would like to see her come. Are you going to show us?"

A few more people look our way, and I see some nods. A dawning horror blooms in my stomach. Matthew said that I wouldn't be having sex in public, but he didn't say that I wouldn't come, and he just said that he likes to show me off. I'm not sure I can do this. My heart starts to pound and I can't seem to catch my breath through the corset. "Yellow," I whisper. "Yellow. Yellow."

Matthew doesn't respond to Chris. Instead, he's out of the chair and in front of me instantly. He searches my eyes. "Hold your breath and count to five."

I do.

"Again."

I do.

"Again."

And the corset eases, I can take a full breath. "What's going on in there?" he asks me.

"So many people. Please, don't make me come in front of them." Sudden and unexpected tears spring into my eyes. "I know what you say goes, but please."

His hand comes up and cups my face, and he kisses me softly. The kiss feels like calm safety. "Breathe," he says softly. "Are you asking this because you're embarrassed or because you're scared?"

The answer is easy. "Scared."

He searches my face again. "You don't mind being watched, but you're scared that I would listen to what Chris wanted instead of what I thought was best for you."

The tears spill over my eyes as I nod, relief flooding cold and swift through my chest that he understood. He gathers me closer, pulling me against his chest even with my arms still bound. "Let me be very clear," he says softly. "I take my responsibilities as a Dom very seriously, and my responsibility is only to you, not to giving my friends treats. And while I think that you might enjoy a little bit of exhibitionism, it wasn't my plan for today."

There's a kiss on my forehead.

"Thank you, Sir."

"Don't thank me yet," he says. "I'm not going to force you to come, but until everyone leaves, I am going to display you."

Matthew wipes away the remnants of the tears, and even though I don't like the thought of being display, that terror that was constricting my chest is gone. "Display me."

He helps me to my feet and pulls me over towards the door. "You didn't mind being seen," he says. "I felt you after I kissed you. You looked around and saw everyone watching, and you relaxed. So while everyone leaves," he says, unhooking my cuffs from behind my back, "You get to be everyone's goodbye treat. Looks only, no touching."

He re-hooks my cuffs in front, and then to a chain that's dangling from the ceiling. The chain retreats, pulling my arms upwards until they're stretched and I'm on my toes. Matthew bends down brushing kisses across my skin as he moves my legs, wrapping them in cuffs that spread them open. I feel precarious and open, and somehow, strangely, totally safe. His words about being only responsible to me keep echoing around my head.

He steps behind me, and I feel the stays of the corset loosen. "Everyone will get to see how fucking sexy you are," he says, lips against my skin. "And when they're gone, we get to play."

There's a carnal darkness in his words that makes me shudder, and I want it. I want him to make me come. The corset keeps loosening and I take the deepest breaths I have in hours. He gets to the bottom, and it slips free, my nipples hardening suddenly in the cool air. The tiny vibrator starts again, softly. Almost barely there, but I can feel it.

Matthew steps in front of me with a wicked grin. "This isn't enough to get you off, but I think it's enough to keep your mind on what's in store for you later." And then he's gone, circling the room and speaking softly to every couple who start wrapping up whatever their doing and heading out the door.

Chapter 9

I don't know what Matthew said to them, but one by one the people in the room leave, and as the pass, they look at me. I'm distracted by the quiet and insistent buzz in my panties, but everyone says something. Whether it's a compliment on my body or on my service or an encouragement in my submission, but the time that Chris and Jenny are leaving, I'm flushed with all the praise as well as the slowly, slowly building pleasure at my core.

Chris stands back and let's Jenny approach me. "I know you're new to this," she says, "but I wanted to tell you that you're doing really well. And if you have anything you want to talk with another sub about, ask Master Matthew to give you our number. I'd be happy to talk with you."

“Thank you,” I say, still glazed and breathless.

They leave, and I feel the sudden absence of people, and I feel Matthew’s focus snap to me. We’re alone. Really alone. And now he can do whatever he likes to me. Anxiety and anticipation mix in my stomach, and I look to find him near the windows, watching me.

“I’m deciding what I want to do with you,” he says, answering my unspoken question.

I’m suddenly acutely aware of my own near-nakedness, and how he’s staring at my breasts. The vibration in my thong intensifies and I gasp. “Now that everyone is gone, I plan on making you come,” he says. “A lot. And also keep you from coming. A lot.” The vibration keeps building as he walks toward me, slow and steady. “Eyes on me, Emma.”

"Yes, Sir."

His hand reaches me first, stroking from my shoulder, down to my breast. I arch into his hand, further off balance, and the vibrations go up again. Both his hands are on my breasts now, rolling my nipples through his fingers. Again and again almost to the point of pain, but not quite. My brain is short-circuiting and I'm hyperventilating. My pussy is dripping with need. "Please. Please. Please." The word is a chant and a prayer and the only word in my brain because I've been turned on for hours and this orgasm is the only thing I want right now.

Matthew grabs my ass and pulls me against his body so I can feel his erection, and the vibration ticks up one more time. "Yes," he says, and he kisses me.

I come apart in his arms, the orgasm shuddering through me like an earthquake.

Quiet shaking at first and then a roar and earth-shattering pleasure. It crackles up my spine and through my mind and it's dripping down my legs and I can't breathe. It's even better than the first time.

It's hard to come down from that. Matthew lets me down from the chain and steadies me while he releases my feet and scoops me off them. I'm carried across the room and laid on a padded surface. "What are we doing?" I ask, and my voice is rough with my orgasm.

Matthew just smiles. "More."

The rest of the lingerie is slipped down my legs, and I feel him move my ankle and I hear the clink of metal again. I try to move my leg, but it doesn't move. My mind is suddenly clear again, and I sit up as he binds my other ankle. "You're tying me up again?" It makes me more nervous than I want to be, even though I know he won't hurt me.

"Problem?" he asks, raising an eyebrow.

Wrapping my arms across my chest, I look down. The words are up on my lips, and he did ask for honesty. "It wasn't sex before."

The table splits between my legs. Matthew pulls the wings apart so my legs are spread and he steps up between them. Since his cock is perfectly aligned with me, I know exactly what this table is meant for. "When I asked you what turned you on about Karen and Greg, you said you didn't know."

"I don't."

Fingers tease the skin of my waist. "I think you do, and don't want to admit it. I think," he says, bending to lick the skin at my collarbone, "that seeing Karen bound, helpless and vulnerable, made you wet, and made you want to feel the same way." I look away toward the windows and the setting sun, and don't answer. "Do you want to have sex with me, Emma?"

"Yes."

Silence.

"Yes, Sir."

I hear the hiss of fabric, and look back to see Matthew's shirt slip to the floor. I'm completely distracted by his body. I'd felt it against me, but I was so focused on other things that I didn't realize how…built he is. Muscles on top of muscles. Muscles in places that I didn't realize you could have muscles. I reach out to touch him and he catches my hand. "You have a couple of options, and I'll be nice and let you choose."

I swallow. "Okay."

"First option. You admit that you *are* a sub, that you want this and me, and you lose the bet."

An unexpected laugh bubbles up through

me and it erases all the tension that I've been feeling. "No way."

He smiles, too. "I didn't think so. Second option, you use your safe word and we say that we've had enough for the night."

My stomach falls, and I shake my head.

"Okay, then since you're still my sub for the evening, you *will* choose one of these." There's power in his voice now, the kind that makes me straighten up and listen. His fingers tighten on my waist, another reminder of how close we are. "You will lie back, accept the restraints, and I will fuck you." Matthew's voice lowers and tingles roll down my spine. "I will take you with my mouth, my cock, and I will demonstrate how very pleasurable being restrained can be. Or we'll leave this room and go to my office. You'll spend the night at my feet, and you'll be put to good use. Just like Jenny."

My core clenches, and I realize what he

means. He's going to have me sit under his desk until he tells me to suck his cock, and then he'll have me suck him and he'll control my breath just like I watched. My breath speeds up and that thought is terrifying and strangely thrilling. But I can't do that. I'm not a person who sits at someone's feet. I'm not a pet. "The first one," I breathe.

"Interesting," he says. "Maybe we'll try that other one another time."

I can't say 'Yes, Sir.' I refuse to admit that it might be exciting. Matthew unbuckles his belt and lets his pants fall to the floor, and then his boxers, and then I stare at him. He's big—erect and jutting towards me. I'm wet again, wanting it. Wanting him. "Lie back."

Nerves are singing in my gut, but I do. He makes quick work of my wrists, and I realize that I'm bound just like that girl

Karen, in an X, spread open, unable to move. Matthew leans down and takes my mouth in a kiss. Moving to my neck, I start to feel hypnotized by the feeling of his lips. His mouth covers my nipple and I arch off the table. I'm so sensitive that it feels like his mouth is right on my clit, and he chuckles at my reaction. "So responsive. This is going to be fun."

"Yes, Sir."

He moves to my other breast, and I fight the restraints, wanting to bring him closer. "What are your safewords, Emma?"

"Red. Lemon."

"Good." He scrapes his teeth across my skin and I moan. "This is more than about sex, you know. When a sub is restrained, everything is taken away from you. I have all the power, and I make all the decisions. Nothing is left but your honest reactions, and the more vulnerable you are, the more powerful your response."

I can barely focus on his words because he's nipping down my stomach. Close, close, closer to exactly where I'm dying for him to be. His tongue traces the outside of my belly button, and down into the crease of my hips. And then he's there and *oh god* just the tip of his tongue on my clit takes me there. I'm dying for more. I want to be over the edge. I want to pull him closer but I can't move. I try to lift my hips closer to his mouth, but he holds them flat, teasing me with the slightest touch, and no more. Taking his time, however he pleases.

I will only get what he gives me, and that realization sinks in, settles over me like a blanket. My mind quiets, eases, and the pleasure sparking from his tongue comes to the forefront.

"You may come once," he says, and then he devours me. His tongue licks into me, and I gasp, orgasm exploding from the unexpected onslaught of sensation. The scrape of teeth and flicks of his tongue taking me higher and higher, and then he seals his mouth over my clit and sucks deeply and I come again. There's no way to stop it. My body shudders and I can feel myself gush into his mouth. I feel the way he laps it up, dipping inside me.

Little spasms jump across my body as I come down from the high, and Matthew leans up to kiss me. I can taste myself on his lips and I'm wet all over again. "You're delicious," he says against my lips. "Another day I might spend hours between your legs."

I can't say anything. I just visualize that —bound to a table while he feasts on me, orgasm after orgasm, unable to stop, unable to stop him. Just that image almost sends me over again. He sees it on my face and smiles. "I see you like that idea."

"Yes, Sir."

He stands and disappears from my view, and I hear a drawer opening and closing, the tinkle of metal and the crinkle of a condom. "How good do you feel right now?"

"I feel pretty fucking good," I say, adding, "Sir," at the last second.

He laughs, and I'm mesmerized by the sight of him rolling on the condom. It makes him look even bigger, and I squirm on the table, wanting to reach out, and the realization that I'm at his mercy almost flattening me again. Once the condom is on, he holds up a strange metal contraction I don't recognize. "This is a nipple clamp."

Those words hit me like a splash of cold water. "What?"

"Sometimes, the tiniest bit of pain adds to the pleasure. Remember, I told you that I'm not a sadist. I do not cause pain for the sake of pain, but this, I think, you will like."

He drapes the chain across my stomach, and the cold sends goosebumps skittering across my skin. He looks down on me from between my legs. "Are you scared?"

"Yes, Sir."

"Do you trust me?"

Amazingly, I do. "Yes."

"Perfect," he says, and he slips into me. I groan, pleasure spiking through me, and I've never felt this full. And I realize as he begins to move that he's not even all the way in.

"Oh god," I say out loud, "that's good."

He pushes slowly in until I feel his balls settle against my ass, and I feel like I can breathe even less now than when the corset was on. "How many times did you come while my mouth was on you?"

"Two," I answer before I realize that's not the right answer. My eyes fly open and I find him grinning.

"I look forward to punishing you for that

later."

"I couldn't help it. There was no way to stop it."

Matthew pulls out a little and thrusts back in. "I'll think about that, but right now you don't have permission to come."

I moan as he thrusts in again. "Please."

"No, especially if you forget your manners."

"Please, *Sir.*"

There's that wicked smile again. "No."

And then he begins to fuck me. He fills me up again and again, and every grind of his hips against mine drags against my clit and takes me higher, until I'm moaning with every thrust and I'm begging him to please please please let me come again. And just when I think he might say yes, he stops.

Just stops. In the middle of sex. "What?"

The chain slithers against my stomach and I freeze, my pussy clenching around his cock. A deep, carnal laugh comes from Matthew. “Feel free to do that again.”

His lips close over my nipple, nipping and licking until it’s hard and I’m shivering. His breath cools my skin, hardening it even further, and then there’s a sharp pinch and I glance down to find the clamp on my nipple. The sharp throbbing spreads, and then it morphs into heat as his mouth closes on my other breast, repeating the process.

Matthew lifts the chain towards my mouth. “Open.” I do, and he places the chain between my teeth. “Don’t let go.”

The chain is pulling up on my breasts and it hurts. Not bad, but just enough to remind me that they’re there. To remind me that I didn’t *choose* to put them there. That I’m bound, and just then Matthew pushes my legs further apart. Oh god. He moves again, and this position is tighter, fuller, and I can’t say anything with the chain between my teeth. I can't think. Pleasure builds, and my mind goes quiet again. There's nothing but the pleasure and the pain as my breasts bounce with every thrust.

That spark of pain flies down my body, adding to the edge of my pleasure, and I find my body is moving on its own. I'm writhing just like Karen did and I can't stop. I want more. More. I need to go over the edge and take him with me. "Please."

"No." He cuts me off before I even finish the word. I'm on the edge, but I hold on for dear life. My hands are fists, my back arching, and I think I might be screaming. Matthew slows, easing in and out with lazy strokes, and the urgency fades. I sink back onto the table, frustration ringing in every cell from the loss of that pleasure.

"You've never edged before, have you?"

I lock eyes with him, shake my head no.

"Where I push you to the edge, over and

over again. Never letting you go over until one big, final climax."

Oh god. I don't know how much more I can take. I'm going to go over sooner or later. It's too big, too good, too much pleasure. He pulls out all the way and thrusts in to the hilt and pleasure rockets up my spine. I'm not going to last, I know it. My body remembers where it left off, and I'm right there again. "Sir," I say, my mouth struggling to form the words around the chain. "I'm not—I can't—help…"

He reaches down and strokes his fingers across my clit. "Come now."

The next thrust breaks me apart. I scream, body straining against the cuffs, pleasure blossoming through me like a flame. Matthew doesn't stop, and every move sets off more embers that land, setting my nerves on fire. I come twice. Three times because he doesn't stop, and I hear him groan, feel his cock jerk inside me as he comes.

His hips move slowly, bringing me down gently, and sending sparkles spiraling through my body. He's still inside me as he leans over me, releasing one of the clamps, and I cry out at the pain as all the blood rushes back. He sucks my nipple into his mouth again, smoothing the pain and turning it into a gentle throb. "Get ready," he murmurs seconds before he releases the other one. He holds me as the pain recedes, kissing me on the lips, the collarbone, the cheeks.

Whatever tension was left in my body is gone, and I'm barely holding on to consciousness as Matthew pulls out and takes care of the condom, and comes to release me. I feel him lift me off the table, and I can't help but relax against his chest as he carries me away.

***

It's dark when I wake up, and there's skin under my cheek. Out of the window of my bedroom, moonlight is shining down on the bed. I take a deep breath and try to sit up.

"You're awake."

"I didn't even realize I'd fallen asleep."

I can hear his smile. "You had a big day. It's not uncommon. How do you feel?"

"Still sleepy."

He laughs softly. "I meant about what happened."

"Oh." I let my mind look over the memories of everything. "I don't know."

Matthew slips out from underneath me, and then suddenly I'm pinned under his body. I can barely see his eyes in the dark, searching my face in that earnest way that he has. "Don't lie to me."

I shake my head. "I have to talk about it?"

"Yes, you do. I told you before, communication is a big part of this."

"Okay." I swallow. "I…had a good time…but I can't say that the reason I had a good time was because I was tied down or because you're just very, *very* good at sex."

"Why couldn't it be both?"

"Because I'm not this girl, Matthew. I've worked hard to be free, to not have to rely on anyone. I don't sit at people's feet; I don't let people boss me around."

I see a ghost of a smile in the dark. "I guess we're not quite there yet."

"Not quite where?"

"I've been trying to explain, but maybe I haven't been painting a clear picture. This isn't about me bossing you around. This isn't about me taking something away from you by force—it's about letting someone take care of you. Being a Dom isn't always sex, it's me making sure you drank water at the wedding. It's checking your car to make sure the tires aren't bald. And when you submit, you're letting go of some of the worry that comes with all of that. It's letting someone protect you."

I bite my lip, hoping he can't see it in the dark, because that does sound nice when he puts it like that.

"And, of course," he says, pressing a kiss to my lips, "it's a little bit about bossing you around."

I laugh, and I think about actually doing this willingly. What would that be like? I need to know what he expects when it comes to that, because he said there are so many different ways to do it. "How would you do it? If you were in a relationship with someone?"

"Hmmm…" the hum of his voice

resonates from his chest into mine, and the warm weight of his body is lulling me back to sleep. "I'm not strict the way some Doms are. There are a lot more layers to the scene that it would take more time to explain. But some people do it all the time. The sub is always on her knees, always naked, always in active submission. Some people are only Doms in the bedroom. Outside they're equal partners, and once the doors close there's a power exchange. I'm somewhere in between."

"How so?"

I can feel him getting hard against my hip as he speaks. "I don't want a woman who's always crawling behind. I want someone I can spar with; someone I can enjoy as an equal when the time calls for it. But I also like to have a sub at my feet sometimes. To have her on her knees under the table sucking my cock. To have her walk around in underwear I choose or naked and kneeling and waiting for my instruction."

"How would you figure out what time is which?"

"Negotiating," he grins. "I imagine that it might start with set times of day, and as the relationship progressed, hopefully we'd know each other and our boundaries well enough that we would know without having to lay out a timetable."

I nod. I don't know what to say to that. It seems logical and almost normal, if you can really call this normal. I can actually see it, the way it would work, this kind of dynamic unfolding in a natural way, figuring it out as you go. But that thought is too nerve-racking for me to follow through, so I don't. Instead I reach down to touch him where he's hard, to distract him and to distract me.

Matthew catches my wrist underneath the blankets. "Oh no. No more tonight. You're going to need your strength for tomorrow. And Sunday."

"But we could feel good now, *Sir.*"

"And I'm telling you no, *sub*."

I sigh, not wanting to be alone with the thoughts that he's put into my head. But to my surprise, he leans down and kisses me. Deep and soft and arousing. "Sleep, Emma. I'll see you in the morning."

He starts to stroke my skin, and the touch is soothing. And even though seconds ago I was going to try to seduce him, I find my eyes closing. I follow his command, and I drift off into sleep wrapped in his warmth.

Chapter 10

I come awake the way you come awake when you're on vacation: slowly, groggily, with the knowledge that you don't have to do any work. It's bliss.

The sun is streaming in, and from the angle, I guess that I've slept in way later than I usually do. But that's okay, it's Saturday, right? I roll over and find the bed empty even though I never felt him leave. There is, however, a present with a note. I finger the pile of black material and find it soft and silky. The note is made of that neat, efficient handwriting that I now think I would recognize anywhere.

Put this on and meet me in my study.

-Sir

The fact that he signed it 'Sir' makes me shiver. If I had to guess, he doesn't want me to come to his office to chat over breakfast again. I shower and notice I'm sore almost everywhere, but it's not a bad aches. It's the kind that comes after a satisfying day at the gym. I've heard other women talk about being sore after sex in a good way, but I've never had that. I stifle a giggle—I'll have plenty of good sex stories when I leave here. No more feeling left out of that party.

The conversation that we had last night, now that it's daytime and I'm thinking clearly, I'm not sure why the life that he described seemed so plausible. Matthew is a good man, and I think any woman would be lucky to have him. But you don't build a relationship on inequality and the belief that one person is less than the other. There's a whisper in my gut that says that I'm being stubborn, and that's not what I meant, but I shove that whisper down. It's not what good relationships are made of.

I do my make-up and hair again. Matthew didn't tell me I had to, but I don't want to walk into his office looking like I just rolled out of bed. Then again, there might be a certain appeal in that…

The lingerie he left is simple: a plunging black bra and black boy shorts. The black is stark against my skin, emphasizing how little it covers. If I didn't already know what he did for a living, I might think he has a future as a fashion designer, based on the fact that he seems to be able to pick things that are spot on for me.

Wandering out of a bedroom in underwear in a house that isn't mine is still a little weird for me, but I do it. I retrace my steps to the main entry and try to remember where his study is. I think it's in the opposite direction from my bedroom. I'm barefoot, and I make almost no sound moving across the floors, and for a second it feels like I'm in a mystery story and I'm looking for clues in the giant, abandoned mansion.

With that in mind, I jump when a woman in black jeans and a black shirt comes around the corner. I gape, because other than the guests yesterday, I hadn't seen anyone in the house. But the woman doesn't miss a beat. "Good morning, Miss Emma."

"Good morning?"

"I'm Julia, one of Mr. Forester's staff. Are you looking for him?"

She points further down the hallway I was walking. "End of the hallway and take a left. I'm sure he's expecting you."

I blush because I'm in my underwear, and she doesn't even blink as she walks past me on whatever task she was given. Not sure why I didn't think he had staff. I suppose it makes sense—that immaculate breakfast yesterday didn't appear out of nowhere, and unless he has a lot of time on his hands, he didn't cook it himself. Besides, with the animals he keeps and a house this big, of course he has staff.

When I reach the end of the hallway, I hear his voice from behind a door that's open a crack, and I do recognize it. But I probably would have wandered around for a while first. I push open the door, and find a very different Matthew. He's on the phone with his back to me. He's in a t-shirt and jeans and the casual look suits him. Those jeans aren't hiding his spectacular ass.

He smiles when he sees me, and gestures for me to wait. I do, and I look around more thoroughly than when he brought me on the tour yesterday. The windows in the office overlook the back of the property, and it's a hell of a view. Built-in bookshelves are lined with leather bound books. I see every subject imaginable from the predictable books about animals to books on history and music. There are comfortable chairs and a fireplace, and I can see him sitting in here reading a book, perfectly content.

If he had his way, he'd be sitting with a woman at his feet. God knows what she'd be doing. I ignore the image of myself there, maybe reading a book of my own. That image makes me hesitate, because I don't know how it makes me feel. Part of me wonders if would really be that bad? And instantly the other part of me roars that it's not okay to even think about that.

Matthew finishes his conversation and I hear him hang up. "Good morning."

"Morning," I say, turning back to him to find him smiling.

"I had a supply issue in Montana. Otherwise, believe me, I would still have been in bed with you."

I let a small smile through. "I ran into Julia."

"Oh," he says. "Sorry about that, I should have warned you. My staff are all either involved in the lifestyle are fully aware of my involvement. On the *extremely* rare occasion I host submissives, they all know that they're to treat them with the same respect that they treat me."

"They're used to people walking around in their underwear?"

He chuckles. "I wouldn't say they're used to it, but Julia is a Domme, so it's not anything she's unfamiliar with."

"It's so…weird."

Matthew raises an eyebrow. "Of all the things that have happened so far this weekend, that's the one that's getting to you?"

"I guess," I shrug. "It's like the things

that are just short of normal that are the most jarring."

"I can understand that," he says. "Speaking of normal, I think your morning has been a little too normal today." He nods to the center of the open space in front of his desk. "Kneel."

My stomach drops. "Really?"

He doesn't say anything, just stares, and I find myself moving, sinking to my knees under the weight of his gaze. I rub my palms on my thighs, trying to work out the nerves. "Good," he says, "now we'll work on your position."

"Position?"

"Some Doms have a list of known positions that they teach their subs, so that they can have a shorthand of when and how the sub behaves. I don't do that, but I do like the traditional submissive kneeling position. I find it beautiful and graceful. Knees further apart."

I widen my knees as he comes to stand in front of me.

"Wider. Until your toes touch." I do, and he reaches out, fingers grazing the back of my neck. "Lift through your spine to here, and bow your head. And finally," he crouches down and takes my hands, "palms up on your thighs."

He straightens, and I hold the pose. "It doesn't feel natural," I say.

"It's not supposed to. As a sub you would practice it more and it would become easier, but it's designed to remind you of your position. And, if you were naked, it would allow me to see if you were wet."

Chills run down my spine. He's right. In this pose, with my eyes on the ground, it's like I can feel the dynamic stretching between us. In this position—in these clothes—it's impossible not to acknowledge what I'm offering to him. My heart is pounding in the silence, and I'm glad I'm wearing clothes because I *do not* want him to see that I'm wet. I don't want to think about why, either.

"For the remainder of your time here, this is the position I want you in if I ask you to kneel."

I swallow. "Yes, Sir."

There's a metal clinking, and I look up to see Matthew unbuckling his belt. I don't move, and he pulls out his cock, already erect. Up close it looks bigger, and I can't ignore the wetness I'm feeling now.

"If I hadn't been rudely pulled away this morning, I would have added another expectation to our conversation last night."

I glance between his eyes and his cock. "You mean…"

"That's right. Every morning before I leave the bedroom—my cock between your pretty lips. I wouldn't care if you were on your knees, or you were under the sheets, or if you were underneath me while I fucked your mouth. But it would be every morning, and I think you would enjoy it."

I raise my eyebrows. "Really?"

Matthew grins. "Keeping your Dom happy can be very rewarding." I'm about to ask him what kind of rewards he has in mind, but he beats me to it. "Open."

I hesitate. I know the door is open behind me, and I don't want Julia to see me on my knees with Matthew's cock in my mouth.

"Emma, open your mouth."

I do, and he slips his cock inside.

"I know you're new, and I'm patient, but I'm tired of repeating commands to you. The next time I have to repeat something, you'll be punished. You have your safewords if you need to use them. Now suck my cock."

His words ring straight through me, and I

don't hesitate. I plunge my mouth onto his cock, letting it fill my mouth. He's hot, pulsing, hard, and it's hard to fit him because of his size. I've never felt comfortable with my oral sex skills, and I can't help but wonder if I'm doing it right, if I'm doing what he likes. I mean…I know he's hard, but what if what I'm doing isn't turning him on more?

Matthew's hand is in my hair and he pulls me off of him. "Where did you just go?"

I blink, startled. "I…"

"It's like you disappeared."

"I was worried that I wasn't doing it right. I've never been good at it, and I didn't know if you liked it."

He doesn't smile or laugh. "You were worried?"

I blush. "Yeah."

"You don't have to. Part of this is you

not having to worry. If I want you to do something differently, I will tell you. If I want you to do something specific, I will give you instructions." Now he smiles. "I don't have you here out of charity, Emma. I like you. I'm attracted to you. I like fucking you, and I like dominating you. My cock has been hard all morning thinking about this."

"Oh." It's the only word that comes into my head, reassurance soothing over me like a cool breeze.

"Now hands behind your back, and suck my cock. And Emma," his fingers tighten in my hair, "you will swallow."

"Yes, Sir," I say, locking my hands together and taking him into my mouth again.

I stroke him with my tongue, taking him as far as I can again and again. Swirling my tongue around his head, I tease the underside and taste the salty cum already leaking from him. I move faster, bobbing up and down and creating as much suction as I can.

Matthew's fingers are in my hair again, and his voice is low and rough. "Slower." He tugs on my hair, and begins to guide my pace. I let him, and I get a feel for the rhythm that he wants. I know that I've got it right when I hear his breath hitch and his cock jerks between my lips. He groans, and I think it might be the sexiest sound I've ever heard. It goes straight to my pussy, and I have to clench my hands into fists to keep from reaching for him.

He tilts my head and suddenly I'm taking him deeper and it's harder to breathe. I didn't know I could take this much of him, and my mouth feels stretched. The tip of his cock touches the back of my throat, and I jerk back against his hand. Matthew pulls me off his cock and lifts it away from me. "Open."

I do automatically, and then his balls are in my mouth. Our eyes are locked, and again I feel that dynamic tension between us. In this moment, I'm on my knees not because I have to be, but because I want to be. I want to make him feel good. I want him to come, and I want to taste it on my tongue. I suck on his balls, and I hear his breath hitch again. "I don't think you know how hot you look right now."

I can't speak to answer him, but my body responds to his words, heating up and the slickness between my legs growing more apparent. "We spoke yesterday about how to trust your Dom, even with your oxygen. Can you do that? Can you trust me?"

I nod, still sucking.

He guides me back to his cock, and I'm full of him again. I close my eyes, surrendering as he guides me down until I think I'm at my limit. And then he guides me further and the tip of him slips into my throat. I can't breathe, and panic rises swiftly. My hands fly from behind my back and I try to push him away, but I hear his voice. "Trust me."

He lets me go and I heave in a breath. I try to calm my gasping, and Matthew's voice is calm. "Were you actually out of breath? Or were you scared about running out?"

I think, and I know what the answer is even if I don't want it to be the answer. "Scared, Sir."

"Take a deep breath, and try again. Trust me to see what you need."

I look up at him, and see nothing but confidence and reassurance. Hauling in a breath, I open my mouth and he slides in again. All the way, to the place where I can't breathe, and further. "Trust me," he says, and I realize that I do. He's not going to hurt me or suffocate me, and this is what he wants. A sliver of tension releases in me and suddenly he's sliding further in because I'm not fighting it. My nose is pressed against the skin of his stomach and through the fog in my brain I realize that I've taken all of him.

Matthew pulls me back and I breathe deep. "Damn," he laughs softly, "I didn't expect that."

"Neither did I," I say, catching my breath and unable to help my grin. "Sir."

I take a breath and he pulls me onto his cock and seconds later I'm pressed against his body again. Matthew groans, a carnal sound that makes me want him inside me more than I can describe. I grab his legs, and he pulls me off his cock. "Behind your back, or I'll tie them there."

I put them behind my back as he pulls me back onto him. He works his way into my throat, and as soon as my lips meet his skin, his fingers dig into my hair and he holds me still. His hips move and then he's fucking my mouth, and I feel that same mental quiet that I felt yesterday. The world shrinks to the feeling of his cock sliding against my tongue and the tightness of him entering my throat. I'm so turned on that I think if he touched my clit I would explode.

Matthew fucks my mouth with shallow strokes, his eyes closed, and I suck him as hard as I can. His hips start to move erratically, quickly driving in again and again and again and he explodes in my mouth. Salt and cream and the taste of man flow across my tongue and I swallow as he continues to thrust. I take everything that he gives me, and I seal my mouth around him, making sure that I don't lose a drop.

He doesn't move for a minute after he finishes, the tip of him still between my lips.

When he finally opens his eyes, they're unfocused, glazed with pleasure. "Show me."

I open my mouth and show him that it's empty, that I swallowed everything just like he told me to, and he smiles. "Good girl."

Warm approval and happiness wash over me like a wave, and I have to look away. Matthew pulls me to my feet and into his arms. I like the feeling of his warmth wrapped around me. "You were excellent."

"Really?"

"I think that might be the best blowjob I've ever had."

Again the wave of approval. I like that I made him feel good, that I'm the reason for his pleasure. It feels good.

"What happens now?"

Matthew sighs. "Now, unfortunately, I have more work to do."

He lets me go, and I try to keep the

surprise off my face. "What do you want me to do?"

"You can have free time," he says, tucking a strand of hair behind my ear. "You are, of course, welcome to stay here with me. Though you'll be kneeling. Or you can explore the house, read, do what you like while I work out this mess."

Kneeling quietly in that painful position or have my free run of the house? "House, please."

"I thought so," he smiles and presses a kiss to my forehead. "I'll have someone find you if I change my mind."

He rearranges himself inside his pants and crosses the room to his desk. I'm almost to the door when he calls my name. There's no amusement there. "If I find out that you put on more clothes, or that you got yourself off, I won't be pleased."

I unsuccessfully fight off my blush from

the fact that he knew I was that turned on, and I hear him laugh softly as I close the door behind me.

Chapter 11

Hours pass slowly in the house. I grab the book I started yesterday and take it to the library. There's a chair in a sunny corner that I noticed on the tour, and I was right that it's the perfect spot to sit and read. I'm approached by some of the staff for lunch, and even though it's weird for me to be in this lingerie, they never act like anything is wrong. Plus, the tea and lunch they make me are absolutely delicious.

Every time I hear footsteps, I'm expecting that someone's going to bring me a note from Matthew with some naughty instruction, but it's never that. I keep thinking about this morning, and yesterday, and with every passing hour I'm more and more on edge. My arousal never decreases, and neither does the fact that I'm so wet I'm constantly aware of it.

When it's time for dinner, I'm so eager to see him and for him to get me off that I'm practically bouncing as I wait in the dining room. But then he doesn't come, and the housekeeper asks if I'd like my food in my room, or maybe in the living room with a movie. I excuse myself, and head for his office. I'm hungry, but I'm more hungry for something else, and I'm not going to get it waiting in the living room with a movie.

The lights are on in Matthew's study and as I push open the door I see that my vision of him this morning was right. He's sitting in a chair next to the fireplace—even though it's too hot for it to be lit—with his nose buried in a book. He looks up when I come in and smiles. "Hello."

"Hi."

"Are you all right?"

I put a bit of sway in my hips as I walk

towards him, "I just…hadn't seen you at all, and I wanted to."

"That's a nice surprise." He tugs me down for a kiss, and when he releases me I'm a little lightheaded.

"So…is there anything you want me to do?"

He laughs. "No, not at the moment." And then he goes back to reading, which I see now isn't a book but looks like something business related.

"Are you sure?" I sink to my knees, making sure I get the position right.

"I'm sure, Emma," he says.

Frustration grips my stomach, and I stand quickly. I feel like there's so much energy in my body that I can't hold onto it all, and I know a really easy way to get rid of some of it, but I'm not allowed to touch myself. Not like that. I walk over to Matthew's desk, and place myself provocatively over the edge of it. "You know, I've always had a fantasy about being fucked on a desk."

His voice is filled with amusement. "I'll keep that in mind." But he doesn't move.

"Why aren't you doing anything with me?"

"Because it's my decision. I can use you or play with you as I like. Or not. But if you ask nicely, I'll consider it."

Anger spikes through me, and my hand lashes out and knocks over a cup of pens. They clatter onto the desk and then onto the floor. Matthew's head whips around, and he sees me and he sees the pens. He sets aside the papers and stands. "Come here."

I do, even though I'm nervous. Because he doesn't look happy. His face is cold, stern, and I don't remember seeing his face like this since I've been with him. Matthew crosses his arms. "Did you do that on purpose?"

I shrug.

"Verbal answers."

"Kind of. It was instinct."

"Why?"

I force out a breath. "Because I've been turned on all day and I didn't come here just to sit around and do *nothing*."

He nods slowly. "Strip."

My blood freezes. "What?"

"Strip. Now. Until I say otherwise you've lost the privilege to wear clothes."

I look down at the floor, shame filling me up to the brim. Not because I'm currently taking off my bra and handing it to him, but because I can feel his disappointment like it's touching my skin. I push the boy shorts off my hips and let them pool around my feet. Then I hand them to him, but I still can't meet his eyes.

"You will go to the playroom and you will kneel. And you will wait."

"How long?"

There's a beat of silence before he answers. "Until I'm ready. As your Dom, it is my responsibility to make sure your behavior and manners are corrected, but also that I never do so while I'm angry or frustrated. So you will wait until I am ready, and then you will receive your punishment."

I swallow, finally meeting his eyes. He raises his eyebrows and I drop them again. "Yes, Sir."

Thankfully, I don't run into anyone on the way to the playroom. Even if the staff are prepared, *I* am not prepared to face one of them while completely naked. Despite the shiver of fear running down my spine, my arousal hasn't dimmed in the slightest.

Maybe there's a possibility that he'll change his mind and fuck me instead of punishing me. There's the tiniest whisper of a thought—that maybe I'll like the punishment. That maybe the reason I'm still aroused is that I want this. But that…can't possibly be true.

The playroom seems impossibly big when I enter it. Alone with the equipment, this seems entirely overwhelming. I find a spot in the middle of the room where there's an empty spot of carpet, and I kneel. I remember his words from this morning, and I know that he's going to see how wet I am the moment he walks in. God help me.

I'm honestly not sure how much time passes between when I kneel and when Matthew enters the room. I can't see a clock, but the setting sun fades and the sky grows dark. When I finally hear his footsteps, my gut tightens with anticipation and fear. His shadow falls across me, and I fight the urge to look up.

"Hands," he says evenly.

I lift them and he buckles the cuffs onto

them and clips them together. He circles behind me and has me rise onto my knees as he does the same with my ankles. Lifting me to my feet, he carries me like I weigh nothing and settles us into the same chair we occupied yesterday.

"Do you understand why I'm punishing you?"

"I knocked over the cup."

He shakes his head. "No. Trust is the most important thing in a Dom/sub relationship, but respect is almost equally important. If you have a problem you want to discuss with me, I'm willing to talk about it, but you don't knock things over or act out. I'm punishing you so that you understand and remember that. The discipline aspect of this dynamic helps both parties purge their emotions and move forward—hopefully without the same mistakes."

I hate, *hate* how much that makes sense. But it does make sense, and acceptance is swift and calming. "What are you going to do to me?"

And just like that, Matthew has me flipped over his knee. "I'm going to spank you. I'm not going to tell you how many times, because part of this lesson is that you need to trust my decisions as your Dom. And also because you need to *accept* my decisions. As the leader, I take responsibility, and you need to believe that I know what's best and am acting accordingly."

His hand smooths over my ass, and I shudder as goosebumps fly up my spine. "And after every stroke, you will say 'Thank you, Sir.'"

"I'm thanking you for this?"

"You are," he says, "for taking the time to correct your actions and invest in this relationship, even though you're fighting it like hell." Matthew sighs. "I don't enjoy handing out punishment. I prefer spanking to be fun, sexy, and pleasurable. This will not be. You have permission to scream, cry, whatever you like."

Fire burns across my ass and I cry out, realizing that it's started. It hurts more than I thought it would, even though his hand is rubbing the sting away. I think I was momentarily blind, and when I blink open my eyes again, a see my hands are balled into fists, straining at the cuffs. "I'm waiting," he says softly.

"Thank you, Sir." I say the words even though I don't mean them.

Another blow. This one in a different place than the last. It burns like wildfire and my cry is louder this time. I grit my teeth and grind out the words, "Thank you, Sir."

Again his hand falls, on the skin at the

top of my waist and my eyes burn. "Thank you, Sir."

We sink into a rhythm, his blows landing slow and steady, with enough time for me to absorb the impact and the pain and work my voice through the thanks, and then again, and again. I don't know how many times, it ceases to matter. Shame and embarrassment well up in me until my eyes burn, and I'm fighting the tears. I know he can hear it in my voice, but he doesn't stop.

Just like he said, there's nothing in the blows of his hand that's angry. If anything, I feel his reluctance as one hand alternately rubs my back and holds me still as he spanks me. If I had just been good this wouldn't have happened. I knew that knocking over that stupid cup of pens would make him angry and I did it anyway. A tear slips out of my eye and I choke on my thanks, but I get it out. Even if it's more sob than words, I get it out.

There's a voice in my head now—not Matthew's—and it's saying things that I've heard before. *Why aren't you ever good like other girls? I swear, any other girl would appreciate what I'm trying to do. I don't know why you think you know better than I do—I know what's best for you.*

Another blow, and I can only gasp, sobs wracking my body now. "Thank you, Sir." But I'm not even aware, because his voice is echoing in my head. *You never listen. You never learn. If you're not going to, I'll find someone who will. Someone who will listen and be good for me.*

Pain explodes through my skin, and I can't hold it back anymore. "I'm sorry," I cry. "I'll be good. I will, please don't leave."

"Last ones, Emma." Quick, fiery slaps to each side of my ass and one blow across them that makes me cry even harder. My chest aches just like it did that day, and I know that I'm not going to come back from it this time. "Please don't leave," I say through my tears. "Please don't leave. I promise I'll listen. I'll be good."

I'm in Matthew's arms and I cling to him. I can't control my breathing, and it feels like the sobs are being ripped from my chest and I don't think I could stop even if I tried. I don't have enough energy to try. He lays me down, and pulls me closer to his chest, and pulls a blanket over our bodies. He doesn't try to stop me, doesn't try to find out why, doesn't do anything but hold me. And I cry until I don't feel like I can anymore, and then a little bit more.

I feel him wiping the tears from my cheeks as I fade into sleep.

Chapter 12

When I open my eyes I feel clear. There's no grogginess, I just come into awareness, and slowly, the memory of what happened comes back.

I'm in a room that I don't recognize, but is clearly a bedroom. It's decorated in shades of deep blue, with dark wood and a simplicity that reminds me of Matthew. This has to be his private room. I didn't see it on the tour of the house, and he must have carried me here after I lost it in the play room. Lamps are casting soft and clear light through the room. It's dark outside, but I don't think that much time has passed. A glance at the clock confirms that it's not that late.

I hear a sound and a door to my left opens to reveal Matthew in nothing but boxer briefs. If I didn't know what he looked like without those, I think this would be my favorite view. "You're awake," he says, a soft smile playing on his lips.

He slides under the blankets of his bed with me, and I gasp as his skin touches mine. I'm still naked, cuffs still gracing my wrists and ankles. "I don't know what happened," I say. "I don't know where that came from."

Reaching out, Matthew runs a hand through my hair. The gesture is soothing, and I arch into it. I love it when people play with my hair. It's been so long since someone did it that I'd all but forgotten how good it feels. No wonder I like it when he guides me using his fingers in my hair. He smiles, repeating the movement, and my eyes almost flutter closed. He could do that for hours and I'd be happy. "Believe it or not, what happened isn't all that uncommon.

Especially with someone as new to submission as you are."

"What was it? It felt…like I was going crazy."

"Do you remember what you said?" he asks, curiosity lighting his eyes.

I think carefully. I remember the pain and the ache in my chest and crying harder than I think I ever have, but…no words. "No."

"At the end you were saying that you were sorry. You promised you would listen, and that you would be good. You asked me not to leave." I stiffen, and I try to pull away from him, to create space between our bodies, but he holds me close. "Breathe, Emma," he says, and I pull in a shuddering breath.

"Before we go any further, let me assure you that I am not leaving. I'm going to stay right here all night. You're not alone."

Those words comfort the irrational panic

that I'm feeling. It doesn't make sense. That was…almost four years ago now. I can't possibly be still affected by that. By him.

"Who left you?"

I look up into Matthew's eyes, those gorgeous green eyes that attracted me to him in the first place. I don't see anger or judgement there. I see…safety. I clear my throat, and it feels rough from my crying earlier. "Jeremy."

Matthew nods. "You loved him?"

"Yes." It comes out a whisper. "I loved him more than I thought was possible. But —" I break off, considering my words carefully, "I know he wasn't a good guy. He didn't hit me or anything, but he never really seemed happy with me." I laugh, even though nothing about it is funny. "It took me a long time to even realize that."

"Let me guess," Matthew says gently. "He told you that you never listened to him." He catches the look on my face and drags his fingers through my hair again. "I heard what you were saying. It's not a far leap."

I nod. "When he left, he told me that since I wasn't going to, he'd find someone that would 'listen and be good for him.' I don't know what it was, what I could have done differently to make him happy. I thought I'd tried everything—"

"Emma," he says, and his voice has that low current of power. "You did nothing wrong. Nothing, do you understand me?"

I bite my lip, nodding. I understand that he thinks that, but he wasn't there.

"You don't believe me, do you." Not a question.

"No, Sir."

He closes his eyes, "And this whole time when I've been asking you to trust me to know what's best for you, you've been reminded of him."

"I honestly hadn't thought of it until last night. Not consciously, anyway."

Matthew leans in and presses a soft kiss to my lips. Slow at first, then deeper, stronger. A flash of heat sears through me and I remember that I'm naked and that he's almost naked and the ways that could be fun. "I'm not surprised you're so resistant to the idea of being submissive. The last man you trusted with that kind of power didn't ask for it. He took it from you, made you feel small and helpless, and then let you fall when you needed him most."

Unexpected tears spring into my eyes, and I blink them away. I think I've already cried enough. Hell, I'm not even sure how I have water left in my body.

"Submission doesn't make you weak, Emma. It makes you strong. A true Dom doesn't take power unless it is offered.

Doms can't exist without the power the submissive gives them. That's why it's so precious, and why anyone with an ounce of sense in their head would never, ever take it for granted."

"It makes sense, and it doesn't," I say, that familiar frustration rising. "On the one hand I can understand, and the other, why would I do that? Why would I voluntarily give power to someone else? Especially when it can make me feel like *that*."

"It can seem complicated," he admits. "There are a hundred reasons to explain how and why the dynamic works with some people and doesn't with others. And it also can be incredibly simple: it can just be something you need."

"Why?"

"Why do people have favorite flavors? Why do some people need to have their office organized in order to function and some like it like a bomb just went off? Why are some people gay and some people straight? Why do I feel most satisfied when someone leans on me? When she lets me decide for her and trusts me to protect her?" He gently taps my forehead with a finger. "It goes deeper than we know. It's a part of who some people are. There doesn't always have to be a reason."

"And you believe, truly believe, that I'm one of those people."

"I do."

I readjust myself, trying to look more resolved. "And what if I am, and I still choose to walk away and let this not be who I am?"

Matthew hesitates. I don't think I've ever seen him do that. "You can," he says. "That's your choice. And you'll be just fine. Do I think that you be happier and more satisfied in a D/s relationship? Yes. But this is not a life or death thing, and it is yours to choose. No one can take that away from you," he says quietly.

"What if I told you that I need to think about that, but I think I'm done talking for tonight."

A slow smile spreads across his face and his hand runs through my hair, tightening, holding my head still. "I'd tell you that as your Dom, I decide when we're done talking. But because you've been very good and honest and vulnerable, I think you should be rewarded."

He flips the covers back, exposing my body. My nipples go hard with the sudden chill. He flips me onto my stomach with that ease that always amazes me, and then my ass is in the air and I try to readjust myself, but my arm won't move. He's attached my wrist to my ankle while I wasn't looking, and now the other one. "Matthew?" I ask, and he makes a low sound in his throat. "That's not my name right now. Try again."

"Sir, why?"

"I'm rewarding you," he says. "Which means you get to have at least one orgasm. That does not mean I'm rewarding you with vanilla sex. It's perfectly clear to me that you respond on a deep level when you're restrained," he whispers against the skin of my neck, "and while I have you here I'm going to take every opportunity to show you that."

I have no leverage, my face against a pillow and my ass in the air because of the way my limbs are locked. It's like I'm being offered to him on a platter, and it makes me shudder. I'm still unsure why I'm attracted to this, but for tonight, I know what he can do to me with his mouth and his body, and I'm going to let him. I want him to make me feel good. For tonight it doesn't have to be about the bet, it can just be about the pleasure of it all.

His hands slide down my ass and I gasp, sensitive to the touch and sore. Fingers drift closer to my asshole, and I tense. He's not going to do that, is he? We didn't talk about that. But he just brushes his finger across it, and I shiver. "If we have more time together, I'd like to explore this. Maybe lock you in a chastity belt for a while so that this is the *only* way I can take you."

"What?" I breathe, unable to help the wave of arousal that falls unexpectedly over me. Then his tongue is there, grazing my ass, feeling so wrong and so right, and my pussy clenches, dampening and giving away the fact that I've gone from zero to sixty in approximately no seconds flat. His mouth moves lower, tasting my arousal, and I arch myself into him. He let's go, spanking me lightly. "Naughty girl, trying to take more than I give you."

Even though it's light, the pain of his hand spreads. I'm going to be sore tomorrow. As he continues to tease me, the pain disappears, morphing and blending with the pleasure coiling in my gut and sharpening it. Matthew drags a finger down my spine. "I'm not going to be gentle," he says. "I'm going to take you, and take my pleasure. Once I'm finished, you'll get your reward."

There's some kind of witty response in my brain, but I don't get to say it. It flies right out of my head as he slides into me in one sure stroke. Oh god, this angle takes him deeper than before, and I'm stretched full of him. The tip of him brushes that place deep inside that almost no one is able to reach and it has me biting my lip. Matthew's palms are on my ass, and he pinches my skin, sending little eddies of pain through me, contrasting with the pleasure of his cock and making it more acute.

"That hurts, Sir."

I can practically hear the smug satisfaction in his voice. "I know."

He thrusts in again and I lose my breath, lose my ability speak or think. I can only feel. I pull at my arms, but the bond to my ankles doesn't give, and pulling on them only spreads my legs wider, offers more of me to him. Matthew grunts with the efforts of his fucking, those small sounds sending sparks across my nerves. Every move he makes brings me closer. I love this. I want more more more more. I squeeze down on him and that just accentuates the way he feels as he drags himself back, pushes in.

I'm mindless with the pleasure, but I also know that it's not for me. This is for him. I'm here for his pleasure in this moment, and I feel a sense of calm, knowing that I'm doing something that makes him happy, gives him pleasure.

He grabs my ass harder, and more pain and pleasure blend together. Suddenly I'm on the edge, crying out as he fucks me, and it feels like an eternity of perfection before I feel him jerk inside me, finishing. Matthew groans, pressing a kiss to the center of my spine. I feel the loss of him and my orgasm as he pulls out of me and takes care of the condom, and then he's right there, flipping me over onto my back, but he doesn't release my restraints.

He opens a drawer by his bed and then a small vibrator slips into my pussy—the kind that has a little loop that circles out and up to cover the clit. Holding up the tiny remote, he grins. I grin too, because this means I'm going to come. But my grin fades when I see him reach for the nightstand and for his phone. He clicks a couple of buttons. "I'm setting a timer," he tells me.

"Sir?" The vibrator clicks on, low but strong enough to make me stop talking. It's on a slow build setting, so the vibration comes in slow waves, building to a higher intensity and dropping back down to almost nothing.

"Ten minutes. Enjoy the vibrator. Scream. Count backwards from one-hundred. Whatever you have to do, but until this alarm sounds, you do not have permission to come."

"Are you serious?" I'm embarrassed by how desperate my voice sounds. He raises an eyebrow. "Are you serious, Sir?"

"I am very serious. And I have no problem spanking you a few more times if you decide to come early."

I don't think that my ass cold take that, and I grit my teeth as the vibrations drive me higher, to the very brink of orgasm and then fade away. I moan, and he chuckles. "No one said that being a Dom wasn't also a little fun."

"You said this would be a reward."

"It is," he smirks. "I could have fucked you and not let you come at all. I could have sent you to bed dripping and desperate, but I'm not. So say thank you."

I glare at him, but I say it. "Thank you, Sir."

"Very nice. Your time starts now."

What? It hasn't started yet? I let my head fall back on the pillow and Matthew laughs, settling into a chair next to the bed to watch. He's still hard, and he absently strokes his cock while I'm writhing around, and I've never felt so sexy. The thought stops me in my tracks for a second. Tied up and being denied an orgasm is the sexiest I've ever felt. Why? What is wrong with me? What is wrong with this? I can't think about it because the vibrations are cresting again and it's everything I can do to stop myself from going over. It's like holding back a wave.

"I can't," I tell him. "It's too much."

"You can. Look at me." I do, and I focus on that hand, moving up and down, teasing himself. "Up here."

We lock eyes, and the vibrations fade. "Why this way?"

"Because right now obeying my will is more important than your pleasure. And because you are submissive, you'll will find equal or more satisfaction in obeying than you will in the orgasm."

"I highly doubt that," I say, my voice strained as another crest of vibrations comes. I look eyes with him again, and his stare gets me through the wave, and then another. Even though I beg him just to let me come, and he says no, looking at him lets me hold on for those fractions of a second before it's too late.

I have no idea if it's just my imagination, but it seems like the waves are getting faster. My hands are clenching and releasing, my muscles shaking, and god I am drowning in the pleasure. I can't see anymore, I'm blind with it, can barely breathe through it, just existing inside of it. I know that I'm almost screaming, a constant, heady plea for release.

And then I hear it, the shrill chirping of what can only be the alarm on Matthew's phone, and I let go because there's no physical way I can hold on any longer. My orgasm rips through me like a supernova, flying higher as that damned little vibrator crests its wave, and I scream. The pleasure is white hot, searing, like every nerve is on fire and I want them to stay burning forever. It doesn't seem to fade.

Matthew's mouth is on mine, and I kiss

him. And I blink my eyes open to see him looking down at me with look that pierces through me—and I know he sees me. All of me. He slips inside me and I gasp, coming again, hard and fast from just the feel of him. Reaching up, I wrap my arms around him—my arms are free! And pull him closer. I can't move anything else because he's cleverly pinned me down with his body.

I smile up at him, because I've never felt like this. I feel…perfect. Warm and aroused and seen and fulfilled and pleasantly blank. My mind is quiet and I'm right here, feeling him as he plunges into me, and again deeper. It's not separate orgasms anymore, just a steady stream of pleasure and I can't keep the grin off my face even while he kisses me.

I go over again just as he does, a groan of effort and pleasure rumbling out of his chest and into mine. He slows, our mouths never separating, and we're breathing together. I feel like I should say something but I can't find any words. It's a long time before either of us moves.

Finally, he takes a deep breath, and pulls free, leaving to take care of the condom. Then he slowly removes the cuffs from my wrists and ankles, massaging the skin as he sets them aside. Leaning close, he presses a kiss to my forehead and scoops me up in his arms. Matthew is still completely naked, and so am I, but he carries me out into the house all the same.

It takes me a couple of minutes to find my voice, and when I do it's rough with sex and tears. "Where are we going?"

"Your room."

"Why?"

He chuckles, and I love the feel of it. "Because if you stay in my room, I will tie you to my bed and I will take you *all night*."

I shiver at his words. “And we’ll both sleep through our last day together.”

Matthew carries me all the way to my room like it’s nothing. I’ve never felt feminine like this. “I like this.”

“What?” he asks.

“The carrying.”

“Too bad,” he says, “I was planning on dropping you in a heap when we got to your room, but now I’ll have to be careful.”

I freeze, “Am I too heavy? I can walk—”

Matthew stops in the middle of the hallway, “No, Emma. I like carrying you. I like the fact that you are *letting* me carry you.”

We finish the trip in comfortable silence. And I’m not sure how he manages it, but he pulls back the blankets and settles me on the bed without even a shiver of effort. I want to ask him to stay, for more of everything, but the warmth of the bed and the way he’s stroking his hand through my hair again is pulling me down into sleep, faster than I thought possible. The last thing I feel is the press of Matthew's lips on my skin as I drift away.

Chapter 13

The sound of my phone ringing wakes me. It seems like it's been years since I've heard that sound. It's in the pocket of my jeans, sitting forgotten in one of the armoires. I stumble out of the bed, trying to reach the phone before it stops ringing. It's Lily.

"Hello?" My voice sounds like it's been blasted with sandpaper. Which, given my activities last night isn't particularly surprising.

"Hi!" She sounds way too chirpy for my brain this early in the morning. Is it the morning? I glance at the clock. Holy fuck, it's almost noon! "I just got back to the states and I wanted to check and see how it's going with Matthew. Your still at his house, right?"

"Yeah, I am," I say. "I'm having a good time. I can understand why you guys do it."

She laughs, bright and happy. "So he was right? You are a submissive?"

"I didn't say that. I mean…yeah, the sex is amazing, but I don't think I can do this. It's not who I am."

"But what if it is?"

I sigh, sitting down on the bed and pulling the blanket up around me. "Did I tell you about Jeremy, Lil?"

"That douche who dumped you? Yes."

"Well, we talked about him last night, and even though I know that Matthew is nothing like him, I'm barely recovered from one man constantly ordering me around and thinking he knows what's best for me. I can't do another."

There's silence on the other end of the phone. "You're right, Matthew is nothing like that. If that's all you think this is, then you shouldn't stay."

"Lily—"

"No, Emma," she says. "I know we're not as close as we used to be, but I know you. And this is my world that you're in. If you're only sticking it out so that you can get revenge on your ex, get out, because Matthew doesn't deserve that."

She's not wrong, but I can't help but think that she's not being entirely fair either. I didn't ask for my past to be brought out of me like a wrecking ball, and now that I'm seeing the parallels, I can't help but notice the tiny grain of sand grating at me, telling me to be careful. That this isn't perfect. That doing this is wrong.

I sigh. "You're right. I'll talk to him about it. But we did make a bet. Matthew knows that, and I want to see that through."

"Please don't hurt him, Emma. I've been thinking about you two, and I really think you could be good for each other."

"I'll do my best," I promise. "Can we spend some time together, soon?"

"Absolutely! But please, promise me you'll try to let go. Explore what this is meant to be and not what you think it is."

I pause, taking a breath. "I will." I hang up, and fall back on the bed. What am I going to do? I feel like I'm being pulled in two different directions. There's turmoil in my gut, but it's not something that's going to be solved by staying in bed. I sit up and slide to the edge of the bed and gasp. Pain bursts through my ass and I leap up to try to relieve it. I pull open the armoire and turn my back to the mirror.

Already purpling bruises cover me, including a very *very* distinct handprint. Oh. My. God. I brush my fingers over the bruises and shiver. I should be furious at him for bruising my ass, but what he did brought me more emotional relief—and later pleasure—than I'd been able to find in a long time. If I knew I was going to have sex like that again, I would go through the spanking again.

That voice in my head rebels against this. This isn't right, that he hit me. But we had agreed that punishment was a part of this. He didn't cross any lines I hadn't already agreed to, and if I had used my safeword he would have stopped. My mind goes blank.

I could have made him stop. I knew I could have made him stop, and I didn't do it. I let him keep going. What does that mean for me? For this?

I look at the bruises again, thinking about the way he grabbed my ass while he was fucking me. How that spark of pain made it so much better, and I'm suddenly wet with the thought that I could have that again. Matthew didn't leave any instructions, so I'm going to put on something. If he doesn't like it, he'll tell me to change.

I flip through the closet, and there's more lingerie than I could ever wear in three days, but it's all my size. I settle on a deep purple babydoll dress. It has a halter top and when I put it on, the skirt just barely covers my ass. Thinking about Matthew seeing me in this makes me grin. The halter pulls up my breasts, almost offering them on a platter. I leave my hair down and I find some light, fruity perfume in the armoire that I put on.

Now it's past noon, and I remember Matthew's words about not wanting to sleep the day away. It's past time I find him. I tiptoe out of my room. I don't know why I think that if I'm quiet that the staff is likely to see me, but it's still true.

Matthew isn't in his study, and he's not in the kitchen. I can't remember the way to get back to his bedroom. I finally find him on the patio, and the sight makes my heart skip a beat. He's playing with two dogs, an adult and a puppy, both golden retrievers. He's throwing a ball for them, and they race to get it and bring it back, both of them practically tackling him when they reach him. The dogs are so happy, tails wagging and smiling wide. He throws the ball again and they run again, the puppy tripping on the stairs going down to the grass. Matthew scoops him up and checks him over while the other dog retrieves the ball.

It's a side of him that I haven't seen before. I knew that he was a good man, and that he worked with animals, but even though I've seen him laugh, mostly I've been witness to the powerful, serious side of him. This soft, goofy, playing-with-puppies side of him is like suddenly seeing who he really is when he's alone. I push open the door because he's already seen me at my most vulnerable, and if I'm going to see him at his, he should know.

He glances back towards the door, and does a double take when he sees me. His smile grows and he puts down the puppy, who rushes down to the grass to play with his friend, and he comes across the patio toward me. Matthew stops just short of touching me. “Good morning.”

“Afternoon,” I say, raising an eyebrow.

“How are you doing?”

I stretch my arms over my head, letting the short length of the skirt ride up and show him that I’m not wearing anything underneath it. “I’m okay. I’m…a bit sore.”

One side of his mouth pulls up into a smile, even though his eyes are glued to my body. “Yeah, I would imagine.”

“You left a handprint.”

“Did I?”

“I shouldn’t be turned on by that, but I am.”

Matthew reaches out and catches me by the wrist, pulling me against him and pressing his lips to mine. My body melts with the memory of everything that comes after this kind of kiss, and he gathers me in his arms. His hands reach my ass and I moan at the sudden pain, and he smiles through the kiss. “Come with me. I have something that will help with the pain.”

“Okay.”

“I should have applied this last night, and…with everything…I lost track. I’m sorry.”

I’m distracted at the feeling of my hand in his, which is shockingly normal. “It’s all right.”

We end up in the playroom, and he leads me over to a padded table. No restraints in sight at the moment. “Up you go.”

I lay on my stomach, and he flips up my dress to explore the bruises. He retrieves a jar of something, and the cold of the cream on my skin gives me goosebumps. "I like seeing my hand on your ass," he says. "It's sexy."

"It may be sexy but it also hurts."

Fingers dip between my legs, and I gasp. "I see it doesn't hurt bad enough that you're not turned on."

"Damn it," I mutter, and a light smack falls on my bruised skin.

"Did you just swear at me?" he asks.

"No."

He starts massaging again. "That's what I thought."

His fingers dig in, and even though it aches, it feels good. And he touches more than just my ass. My legs, and feet, and up to my hips. I'm constantly on edge from the touches that he slips into my pussy, teasing my clit and occasionally dipping all the way inside.

He guides me to roll over and massages my arms and shoulders, and I'm so relaxed that I could go back to sleep again. Until I look up, and I see how hard he is, and he's at eye level. I reach out and grab his belt, undoing it and freeing his cock. I was right, he is hard, and he doesn't stop me as I take him into my mouth. He doesn't give me any commands, and I take advantage, using my hands.

I tug him and tease him, sucking on the head of his cock. I can't take him deep the way that I'm positioned, but I'm going to make him come all the same. The resolution forms in my mind and I'm not going to stop. His fingers are in my pussy again, and I moan around his cock. Two can play at this game. He rolls my clit between his fingers and I arch off the table.

Matthew's hands are magic. I already knew that, but this just confirms it. And oh god—his mouth is magic too. I know this because he's leaned over the table and captured my clit between his lips. His tongue is flicking and I can't focus on anything besides that glorious sensation. I suck his cock harder, no special tricks, just my mouth and my tongue. I try to take more of him, and he takes more of me. His mouth covers me and he licks me in long, slow strokes. He swirls his tongue across me and I jump, my pussy clenches, and I grow even wetter.

I squeeze his cock and he groans. The vibrations of his voice on me are deliciously intimate, and I arch up into him. I want more.

Matthew pulls away suddenly. "Sit up. I don't want to come in your mouth right now."

He helps me sit up and rolls on a condom. And then my ass is at the edge of the table and he thrusts inside me with one brutal stroke and I'm gone. I'm sore and aroused and the combination of sensations is…

I don't have words for it.

Matthew's lips are on my neck, and I'm clinging to him, legs wrapped around while he thrusts into me. This isn't meant to last long. This is fast and dirty and oh god yes, I'm telling him yes and that it feels good. Matthew is grunting with every thrust, fingers digging into my hips, pulling me harder, faster, pressing in deeper. I break open, coming hard as he fucks me, and I feel my orgasm gush over his cock. He growls, and seconds later I feel him come, thrusting in one final time and holding, cock pulsing inside me with his own orgasm.

We're both breathing hard, and he grins as he pulls out and cleans himself up. "Do you want some food? I told the staff to prepare lunch."

I laugh. "Sure."

As we're walking to the dining room, I realize how weird that was. He didn't do any of his Dom stuff. Is it because he's trying to win the bet? Has he changed his mind?

The table is set with an array of sandwiches and drinks, and he sits down. I sit down across from him. "I don't understand."

"You don't understand lunch?" he smirks.

"No," I say. "I don't understand what just happened."

He doesn't say anything, just takes a bite of a sandwich and waits for me to continue.

"You were…nice. You didn't tie me up of tell me what to do. It was just sex."

"I can be spontaneous just like any other person. Kinky people are capable of having regular sex."

"But why?" I ask. "I mean, are you trying to trick me into asking for the submissive stuff so you'll win the bet?"

I see him freeze. He puts down the food in his hand, and when he looks at me, the playful light that was there is gone. "I'm sorry?"

"If I admit that I want to be submissive, you win. So if you *don't* do that stuff and then I ask for it, you win and you get me for a whole month. Was that why you were so nice with the massage and the…" I trail off because the way he's looking at me dries up all my words.

"You think that I'm trying to trick you so that I can keep you prisoner here for thirty days? After everything, that's what you think of me?"

"No," I say. "It just felt…odd."

Matthew sighs and scrubs his hands across his face. "I'm capable of being kind,

Emma. My every action is not build into trapping you into a lifestyle that you don't want. I made the bet to get you here, so that you could see that this life isn't what you thought it was. From the very beginning you've had this…preconceived notion about who I am. And I know that we have a lot of intimacy now, but you don't know that much about me. I thought that after last night you would have gotten a pretty good idea of who I am, but clearly I was wrong about that, and you're wrong about me."

He stands and leaves the room, and the silence is huge. Crap. What on earth did I just do?

Chapter 14

I walk after Matthew, and I can hear his footsteps ahead of me. He's gone back to the playroom, and I find him cleaning the table that we just had sex on.

"Matthew," I say, and he doesn't look at me.

"I like you, Emma." He stops, hands on his hips and looks at me. I can't meet his eyes because I realize that I was wrong before. I wasn't seeing him at his most vulnerable on the patio, I'm seeing it now. "I like you, and I know that I shouldn't, because clearly we don't want the same things. I had hoped…I don't know what I hoped. But if you're only here for the money, then you can have it. I've tried to show you that a Dom/sub relationship is about trust, and if you would really think I'd do something like that then you don't trust me."

"I don't want the money." I don't even realize it until I say it, but it's true. My gut churns and I think I might be sick. I don't like the way he's looking at me, and I don't know how to fix it, but I know that I want to fix it. "It's not that."

"Please, help me understand," he says.

"Last night, when we were talking about my ex—"

"Jeremy," he says, eyes darkening.

I nod. "Yeah. I didn't…I couldn't say how much he hurt me. How I can't trust people. How every time I like it when you tell me to do something I feel sick to my stomach because I think it's happening again. And I know, I know that you're not like him."

"Then why? Emma, I would never do that to you. I would never force you against your will, would never hurt you like that. Why?"

"I don't know," I say.

He takes a step towards me. "Yes, you do. You just don't want to say it."

"No. I've been trying to figure it out for the last three days and nothing."

Another step. "Then tell me why you don't want this. Everything about your reactions when we're together tells me that you're a sub and that you love it. So why do you keep running away from this? Why do you keep pushing it away?"

"I don't know."

"Don't lie to me." Another step closer. "Don't lie."

"Because I don't want to be broken anymore!" The words burst out of me, and the tears follow. "After Jeremy left I was broken for a long time and I still might be broken and wanting this—wanting you—

liking you telling me what to do makes me scared. But I do want it, and that means I must be broken, because a sane person can't keep choosing to give up her freedom." I run out of steam and I stand there, breathing hard, tears streaming down my face, and I know I've shocked him because he doesn't look angry anymore.

He's so close that I want to reach out and touch him, let him hold me, but he doesn't move. "What about Lily?"

"What about her?"

"Do you think she's broken? Do you think that she's screwed up because she married Mark? I don't know how much she's told you about her relationship but he's a stricter Dom than I am. They're in a twenty-four-seven relationship. There's never a moment when she doesn't submit. Do you think she's unhappy? Crazy?"

I take a second and think. Lily has been

talking about Mark for years, and she's never said anything but good things. There haven't been any red flags when I've talked to her, and at the wedding, I've never seen her so happy. "No," I whisper, "I don't think that. Lily isn't stupid. She'd never do something she wasn't okay with."

"Then why do you think you're broken for wanting something that makes you feel good?"

"Because it scares me. What if I just end up in the same place I was?"

Matthew finally closes the space between us, and I hate that the tears flow harder. I thought I had been all cried out last night. I guess I was wrong. The warmth of his arms is so welcome, and I let go. I'm sure I'm his shirt, but I can't stop.

He tips my head back, kissing me softly. "Maybe we should stop," he says. "Maybe you're not ready, and I don't want to scare you away from this life because I calculated wrong."

"I don't want to stop," I say, even though I'm shivering. "Please. Show me that I'm wrong. Show me that I don't have to be afraid of this."

He searches my face, and I don't know what he's looking for. "Are you sure?"

"Please."

Another soft kiss. "You have to trust me."

"I do."

Another hesitation, another searching of my face. I know he's deciding whether or not to move forward, and I desperately want him to. I need this. I need to feel that strange bond between us and be able to let go and let him take control and know that everything will still be okay.

Slowly, Matthew nods. "Strip and kneel."

I don't hesitate, pulling my lingerie over

my head and putting it aside, I sink to my knees in front of him. My head is bowed, and I can't see what he's doing, but he's moved away, and I hear the sounds of equipment being prepared.

It takes a few minutes, and when his feet come to stand in front of me again, I'm relieved. I don't raise my head until I feel a hand on my shoulder. "Stand."

I do, and when I look up I freeze. He's bringing me toward that same X I watched at his party. My heart is beating out of my chest, but I put one foot in front of the other until I'm standing in front to it.

"What are your safewords, Emma?"

"Red and Lemon."

He turns me to face him. "Step back and up."

I step on the platform, and he gently lays me back against the X, which is at an angle now. Just enough that I'm not able to stand.

Matthew buckles my wrists and ankles into the cuffs, and then more straps across my hips and chest. I'm suspended and spread open. "Can you move?" he asks gently.

I shake my head. "No."

"Good. Thank you for trusting me enough for this. And I'm going to ask you to trust me a little more." He places a blindfold over my eyes, and suddenly everything is black and I can't move. My breath goes short and I pull against the restraints. I can't move. I can't *move*.

"Emma," Matthew's voice is calm. "Are you in pain?"

"No, Sir."

"You are safe with me. What are your safewords?"

A way out. I have a way out. My breath calms and the restraints suddenly don't feel as tight. "Red and Lemon."

Fingers drifting across my cheek. "Good

girl."

I hear him step away, and the clicks and the soft scratch of a drawer. Panic suddenly rises again, and I pull on the restraints. "Matthew."

He's instantly by my side, and his hand drifts across my ribs. "I'm here. I would never leave you alone while restrained."

Nodding my head, I haul in a deep breath.

"Let go," he says. "You don't have to worry about choices, because they're not yours. They're mine. What's my name right now?"

"Sir."

"Very good." Another gentle touch across my stomach.

And then another, but it's not his fingers. Tingling, brushing strands tickle down my skin, and I tense. I recognize what it is even if I can't see. It's a flogger. I bite my lip, and

I fight the urge to hold my breath and tense my whole body. “Are you punishing me, Sir?”

A low chuckle, and the soft, warm feeling of his lips on my collarbone. I get chills as he drags his mouth down to my breast, covers my nipple. It hardens under his tongue and he teases the other one until it’s just as hard. “No, Emma. I want to make you scream, but I’m not punishing you.”

His words build heat under my skin, and I try to squirm, and I can’t. The flogger falls across my skin, not hard enough to hurt. It’s a solid pressure that leaves warmth behind as he moves it across me. It falls on my shoulders and my chest, slowly, rhythmically moving lower. Across my breasts, and the sudden bite on my nipples leaves me breathless. But he doesn’t stop, moving lower, the strands wrapping around my ribs. Harder, a little snap, just enough to let me know how much control he has and that he's absolutely in control of how hard that flogger falls.

Slow, dragging strokes across my hips. So close to my pussy, the strands brush the outside. Matthew lets the flogger fall harder on my legs, and I have no idea if he's going to go back to my pussy. I'm fully exposed to him, and if he wants to use it on me, he can. I won't be able to stop him.

I realize that I'm wet at the thought. I'm completely in his hands, and…that's okay. It doesn't matter that I can't see, I can feel the pulse of that between us. Every brush of that leather is an expression of trust between us. I'm choosing to give him the ability to hurt me, and he's choosing to show me that even though he can, he won't. He's showing me that he can see what I need, even if in that moment, it's pain. That he'll give me what I need even if it's something that I wouldn't choose.

The flogger snaps across my thighs, and I gasp. The pain throbs, fading into the heat that's rising all over my body, that's growing in my core where I'm starting to ache. The flogger keeps moving, with harder strokes, and I never know where it's going to land. Shoulder. Breast. Hip. Stomach. Knee.

A finger brushes my pussy and I try and fail to move my hips closer. "You're wet," he says and I can hear the smile. "I like that. Do you?"

"Yes, Sir."

"Open," he says, and his finger touches my lips. I can taste myself on my tongue and my mind goes blank. Fiery arousal burns down my spine and I moan, trying to move, trying to get some relief. But there is none, especially since his clever fingers are at my pussy again, teasing, circling my clit, dipping inside to brush my G-spot. "Please,"

I say.

My answer is the flogger starting up again, and even though I know the blows are harder, it doesn't feel that way. Lines of heat and pleasure spiral from my skin wherever it lands, drawing in close and adding to the pressure of my rising orgasm. I never thought I'd be here, ready to come and he's barely touched me.

"Sir, I need to come." My words are more breath than voice.

"You will," he says.

My hands curl into fists. "Please."

The flogger makes the journey down my body again, and I'm going to come, I'm not going to be able to stop it. Not after he's turned me on like this, teased me. He pauses at my hips. "You have permission to come," he says, voice rough. And then the flogger lands directly on my clit. Pain and pleasure burst through me together and I cry out, coming. It falls again, and again, and I sag against the restraints, the pleasure rendering me helpless.

I hear a thud, and then feel Matthew's fingers. I jump. "Sensitive," he laughs. "I should have used this on you earlier."

There's the soft hiss of fabric and the clinking of his belt and the sound of a condom foil. And then I feel his skin on mine, inch for inch. His cock is rock hard, pinned between our bodies. Matthew is covering my body with his, and he twists our fingers together. "Do you feel that?"

"What?" I ask, swallowing, "Sir?"

"For this moment, you're mine." His lips are at my ear and his voice is so soft it makes me shiver. "You're wearing my cuffs, you're bound to my cross, and you're under my body. There's nowhere to go. I can do what I like to you, and right now, I'm going to fuck you until you're screaming. And then, maybe, I'll fuck you some more."

He slips inside me and my breath is suddenly short, and I become aware of what he's saying. I can feel the cuffs on my wrists and the straps on my skin. I can feel how vulnerable I am on this X, and I can feel the way he's pining me down. He's everywhere, even inside me, and I can't escape. Calm spreads through me like a ripple, thoughts slowing, and I suddenly feel like I can breathe. I'm not afraid, and I don't want to get away. This feeling can't possibly be wrong, and even though I know I have zero power, I don't care. I'd give it all to him again. This doesn't feel like submitting, it feels like the way things should be. It's like a light has gone on in my head, and all the things he's been saying coalesce in a way that makes sense.

Choosing to give him control doesn't diminish me or make me less, it makes me brave. He doesn't have any power that I don't give him, and with the safeword I can always take it back. And deeper, this feeling of vulnerability, or trust, the fact that I can make myself powerless and not be afraid to be hurt…I never thought I'd feel that ever again. It feels like bubbles of joy are springing up underneath my skin, and I'm tearing up behind the blindfold.

"Do you understand?" he asks me.

"Yes, Sir."

"Do you want to use your safeword?"

"No, Sir."

Matthew presses his lips to my cheek. "Good girl."

And then he starts to fuck me. I'm so wet, and I'm so ready, that I'm already on the edge with his first thrust. He kisses me long and deep, and I kiss him back as best I can without being able to move. I dance with his tongue, and I love the way he takes what he wants. He's not afraid to take it because it's his anyway—I gave it to him. I grip his hands harder and I can't keep kissing him because I need to breathe. Every thrust of his cock knocks the wind from me and I never, ever want it to stop.

Matthew's cock is stroking past my G-spot and hitting me hard and fast in that deep place that makes pleasure bloom everywhere and I need to come again. "Please, Sir, can I come?"

"I'm going to ride you hard," he growls. "You have permission to come as many times as you like. And I want to hear you."

He drives in again, and it's like lightning. The orgasm crashes over me hard and fast, and I let him hear me, not quite screaming. I'm certainly not quiet though. The pleasure is there and gone in a flash, but Matthew hasn't even slowed. It feels like that vibrator he left inside me: long, slow strokes that make me shudder with drawn-out pleasure and then speeding up until I'm barely holding on. And over again. And again. I haven't come again even though I'm close, because Matthew knows exactly how far he can push me before he needs to pull back, damn him.

Suddenly I'm blind with light. He's pulled off my blindfold and I can see him, so close and so real, those green eyes watching me. I can look down, just barely, and I see him pushing into me. The sight is like an electric shock to my arousal, and Matthew kisses me as I go over. I scream into his mouth, this pleasure a brilliant, brutal supernova. It sizzles along every nerve. I think I might be lit up, on fire, exploding like a firework and I don't care because it feels so fucking good.

I come down and I'm dragging air into my lungs, gasping. Matthew is still touching me everywhere, and I tighten my fingers around his. "That…was very good…Sir."

"Was it?"

"Yes."

He grins. "Good. I'm just getting started." And then he plunges in again.

***

I lose track of the times I come. Every orgasm bleeds into the next until it feels like my body isn't capable of doing anything but producing pleasure. I'm drunk on it. Blind from it. My voice is hoarse from screaming. My muscles are so limp that there's no way I would be able to stand, even if he would let me. I think we skipped dinner, because it's dark outside. But I'm not hungry—I'm relaxed and satisfied and ready for sleep.

I know that he's cleaning me up, washing me and cooling me, wrapping me in a blanket. He must have unbuckled me because I'm in his arms now, and being carried. I like how familiar this sensation is now, the gentle rocking movement and the warmth of his skin coming through the blanket.

He lays me down on a bed that isn't mine, but is still familiar. We're back in his bedroom, dark and comforting and perfect. I find my voice. "I thought I couldn't sleep in your bed?"

"You're still mine," he says, voice low. "And I want you here, bound and inches away from me." My arms are lifted and I feel the now normal sensation of being locked into cuffs. I try to pull down my hands, and I can't.

"I'm going to stay with you? You won't leave?"

His hand strokes through my hair, and my eyes close. I can feel sleep rising like a tide, relaxation flowing through me. "I'm not going anywhere." The bed dips, and Matthew stretches out beside me, still stroking my hair.

I sigh, smiling, because somehow this is perfect. "Thank you, Master."

There's a soft hiss of breath and my eyes fly open. I'm suddenly awake and I realize what I said. Matthew's staring at me, and the look on his face is one I've never seen before. It's awe and joy and shock all mixed into one. I didn't even realize I was saying it, it just came out.

I'm shaking with the adrenaline that's just been put through my system, and my gut is churning. I'm not sure what this means. Where do we go from here? I'm waiting for some kind of grand speech, or an explanation of what this means, but Matthew doesn't do that. Instead, he smiles. A pure smile that I know isn't one he shows often. It's a private smile, and this one is just for me. He slides his fingers around the back of my neck and tilts my face so that he can kiss me. "You're welcome, sub."

That's all he says, but he never looks away. We stay that way, side by side, eyes locked, until my exhaustion takes over once more and I can't keep my eyes open.

Chapter 15

I come awake slowly for the second time. The first time was when Matthew rolled over me in the night and we had slow, sleepy sex that resulted in a deep and shuddering orgasm that I'm not going to forget anytime soon. One reminder that he could do that—that my arms chained to the headboard allowed him to do what he liked with me, and I was so wet that I might as well have been a faucet.

This time though, I feel his arm draped across my stomach, and then I hear the long, deep breaths of sleep. I shift, rolling onto my side as much as I can to look at him. I feel like I'm stealing something from Matthew, seeing him so relaxed and unguarded. I let my eyes explore, from his lashes—which are long and unfairly pretty—down to the perfect planes of his chest and stomach. If my arms were free I would take this moment to explore with my fingers and wake him up in a manner that I'm sure he would find enjoyable.

My stomach growls. It's been a long time since I've eaten, since our lunch was interrupted by me freaking out. I glance back up to Matthew's face and his eyes are open. He has a playful smirk on his face. "Hungry?"

"It would appear so."

"I'll make sure there's breakfast waiting for us."

I sigh. "Yeah. I suppose I'll have to go after that. I need to get to work. I told them that I'd be late today, but I still need to go."

Matthew props himself up on an elbow. "And why, exactly, would I let you go anywhere? You lost the bet."

"I did not," I say, my stomach dropping.

"Just because I said that last night doesn't mean I lose. I never admitted I was submissive."

"As I recall," he says with a lazy smile, "You said that letting me tell you what to do scared you, but that you wanted it."

I freeze. Crap. I did say that.

"Which according to our bet makes you mine for the next thirty days."

He starts kissing my neck, and even though it feels amazing, my anxiety is spiking. "Matthew, I made this bet never thinking that I would lose. I said it, and I admit that you win, but I can't stay. I don't have thirty days of vacation and I can't lose my job."

"You're not going to, it's already taken care of," he says, reaching up and freeing my arms from the headboard. He doesn't give them back to me though, clipping my wrists together.

I look at him expectantly. "Would you like to share how? Because I'm freaking out. A lot."

Matthew sits back against the headboard and pulls me to him, holding me close. "When we made the bet, I called Jones & Burke and hired them as my new PR firm. I also had them draw up a contract specifying that I would have a personal publicist for thirty days. I haven't activated it yet, but all I have to do is have you sign and call to tell them that I choose you."

I blink. "You were that sure that you were going to win?"

He laughs and it vibrates through my chest. "No, actually. I was going to do it either way. I knew from the moment I met you that you'd be good at your job. You're passionate and opinionated and you're not afraid to tell people they're wrong or try to get them to see your point of view. So even if this didn't work out, I wanted you putting out the good word about my company."

This is the first time in my life that I ever remember being speechless. There are literally no words in my head.

"So," he says, wrapping me tighter, "you can stay here with me and keep up your end of the bargain, while working with me as my personal representative from Jones & Burke."

I swallow. "That's a huge promotion. They're going to be pissed."

He chuckles, "The amount of money I'm paying them, they'll be just fine. But for the next thirty days you're *mine*." Those last words are almost a growl.

"And how exactly am I going to work while I'm here?"

Matthew lays me back so we can see each other face to face. "Just like we talked about. We'll set time limits. For a certain amount of time each day, you'll be my publicist and not my submissive, and the rest of the time I get to do what I like with you."

I think about that. About staying here, being with him, submitting to him all the time. How would that be? Do I really want that? The little voice that's been whispering doubts in my mind the past few days is roaring now, telling me that if I leave I'm a fucking idiot who would be walking away from the best thing that's ever happened. But I don't want to be forced into it, so I have a final question.

"And if I really did want to leave? If I said no to the money but no to the month too?"

His face is guarded, but he doesn't hesitate. "Then you can leave whenever you like. Do you want me to call the car?"

I let myself drift between the decisions

for a moment. And I know. I *know* that if I walk away, I'll always regret it. I shake my head, "No. I want to stay."

He kisses me so fast it makes my head spin. "You have no idea how much I wanted you to say that."

"I'm not going to make it easy on you," I say. "I'm not just going to be a good girl."

The smirk is back. "That's what makes it fun. If I never got to punish you I'd be disappointed." He kisses me again, silencing a retort that probably would have started off a round of punishments. "Now," he says, "before we go sign those papers, we'll be starting that other rule we talked about."

"What other rule?" I can't help but notice that he's hard behind me, and I have no doubt that it has something to do with this rule.

"That every morning before you leave my bed, my cock will be in your mouth. It's the only way to start the day off right."

I raise an eyebrow. "Is that so?"

He sighs with faux drama. "I'm afraid it is."

"Are you going to let me have my hands?" I ask, raising my cuffed wrists.

"And make it easy on you? Not a chance."

"Sadist," I mutter under my breath.

Matthew weaves his fingers in my hair, tilting my head back so that we're eye to eye. "Maybe a little bit, now get down there and suck my cock before I have to punish you for disobedience." He kisses me, and god, I'll be damned but the thought of getting punished is turning me on now.

I smile at him when he lets me go. "Yes, Master." And I sink down underneath the sheets.

Epilogue

Thirty Days Later

It's the last day. Neither of us have said anything about it, but we both know that tomorrow is the day that the bet ends. We haven't talked about what happens, and I haven't wanted to. The last month has seemed like a dream, and I don't think I want to wake up. In fact, all of this has been more like waking up. Like everything before was muddled and hard and this has been bright and easy and perfect.

I'm kneeling in the playroom, naked and waiting. It's been awhile, but I've learned to wait. Matthew was right, the pose doesn't hurt after you get used to it, and it's actually become relaxing. Almost centering. How I got here, I don't think I'll ever know, but deciding to embrace submission suddenly feels like being able to breathe. There's freedom in being able to let go and let Matthew take the lead. Just like he described when he was talking about the life he wanted with a sub, we've found our way, experimenting with boundaries and how much control works for us.

The door opens, and my heart starts to beat faster. He walks over to our chair—the same chair he held me in on that first day—and sits. "Come over here, Emma."

I stand and move, kneeling at his feet. It's all so new, but I'm still amazed at how natural this feels. Matthew leans forward and tilts my face up, giving me permission to raise my head. "I think we need to talk, and right now we're not talking as Dom and sub."

"Yeah," I say, my throat dry.

"You know what tomorrow is."

I laugh nervously. "The date is pretty

much burned in my brain."

"In a good way or a bad way?"

Shifting, I draw myself closer together, suddenly feeling the urge to hide. "I don't know."

He pulls at my hands covering my breasts. "Stop. You know how I feel when you try to hide." I drop my hands. "You're nervous?"

I nod. "Yeah."

"Well," he says. "There are a couple of things that we can do." He pulls me up so that I'm sitting higher on my knees and I'm nestled between his legs. "If you want, all this can end. We can go our separate ways, and we'll think of this as a great memory for the both of us. I don't really want that."

"Neither do I."

He gives me a relieved smile. "Good. Another option is that we can continue on as we are now. Or, you can go home, and we'll work out how this relationship will work living apart. And if those options don't work, we'll figure something else out."

That's a lot of options, and I don't know what would be best. How could I go back to living by myself and also do this? It doesn't seem possible.

Matthew clears his throat, "I know that whatever we choose, it's a big step. But I have some things to say, and they might affect your decision."

"I don't even have a decision yet."

He smiles. "I know, but I'm going to say this anyway." He takes my hands and weaves our fingers together. "When I saw you at Lily and Mark's wedding, I thought that you were beautiful, and I knew that you were submissive."

"You still never told me how."

"It was the way you looked at the kinky couples," he says, pressing a kiss to the back of my knuckles. "Even though you seemed nervous, you didn't look afraid, and there was longing there. You wanted it, even if you couldn't say it."

I glare at him. "Damn Doms."

"Did you just swear at me?"

"No, Sir."

He chuckles. "Anyway. I liked you, and I had fun with you in those fifteen minutes, an even though you wanted nothing to do with me, I thought that if I could get you to admit what you really wanted I could send you on your way, and you'd be a little happier.

"But then you came here, and you were more than I ever expected. You responded so beautifully even when you were fighting me, and I found that dominating you was the most fun that I'd had in a long time, and I didn't want you to go. And after this month, I still don't want you to go."

My heart skips a beat, and I feel myself

go still.

Matthew pulls out a silver necklace. It's delicate and feminine and it pools in his palm like liquid. "I know that I've told you a lot that you're mine, and it was a part of the play. But I really do want you to be mine. My submissive." He stops, and I see emotion spring onto his face. "I love you, Emma. I'm so in love with you, and if I had a choice, I'd never want you to leave. And this," he says, holding out the necklace, "is a collar that would say that."

Matthew told me about collars. About how serious couples in the lifestyle adopt them as a sign of commitment. They're not offered lightly, and in some circumstances are just like an engagement ring. We talked about what it would mean for him, and even though it's not marriage, it's close. A step on the way to getting married. So him offering this to me isn't a small thing.

My mind snaps back to his words and I feel my jaw drop. “You love me?”

“Yes,” he says. “I love you, Emma. More than I could say.”

Joy sweeps through me, and I feel the answering words about to burst from me. “I love you too!” I jump up, and slide into his lap, kissing him. “I love you.”

His arms come around me hard, and he returns the kiss, taking control of it, and I let him. I want to drown in him and never ever leave. Matthew pulls away long enough to look at me. “Will you stay with me?”

“Yes,” I say, pulling myself closer. “I want to stay with you.” And as I say it, I feel that same joy, like every piece of my life just clicked into place. I always want to feel this way. Always.

Matthew sets me down on the ground so I’m kneeling again, now facing away from him. “May I put this on?”

"Yes, Master." I use the title to tell him that I know what this means. That it's serious. And I get tiny goosebumps down my spine while he fastens the clasp.

"Now you really are mine," he says in my ear, voice rough in my ear.

"I know," I say.

"And now that you're not leaving," he says, "we have all the time in the world."

I lean back against his legs. "What did you have in mind, *Sir*?"

"Stay here." Matthew stands and goes to one of the large storage closets and pulls out a whole length of blue rope. "Stand."

We've done this before, and I'm always amazed at the way he can twine rope around me in just minutes. He outlines my breasts and frames my hips, and two strands of rope are running between my legs on either side of my clit. "Sadist," I mutter.

"Keep talking and you'll pay for it later,"

he says, chuckling.

I close my mouth. He wraps me tighter than we've done before, binding my arms to my body. And then he sits me down and binds my legs so I'm bent back over them. There's no way that I can move, and I've grown to like the sensation. It's comforting, and I don't need to know what comes next. All he could have planned is this and I would enjoy it. I have enjoyed it. One day he tied me up with rope and kept me next to him while he worked, and the tension that was between us as he occasionally looked over and touched me, made the sex after absolutely explosive.

He attaches more rope by my stomach and threads it close to my neck and hips. "Something new," he says, lifting me off the floor. "Suspension."

"Really?" My heart rate kicks up a notch. I trust Matthew completely, but the thought of a little rope holding me in the air is still nerve-wracking.

He settles me on the floor again, and the ropes are attached to the suspension rig. "Really," he says. "You like tight bondage like this, and suspension heightens the feeling of helplessness." As if to prove his point, he pushes a button and I'm lifted into the air. My stomach lurches, and I sway back and forth. I don't feel at all like I'm going to fall, but he's right, that helpless, vulnerable feeling that both calms me and sends me to the edge is right there.

I hear the sounds of him getting undressed, and he appears next to me naked and glorious and already hard. He guides my mouth towards his cock. "The perfect height for this."

He slides into my mouth with ease, and he steadies me in the air as he guides my cock into my throat. Every morning I suck his cock, and now I not only know what he likes, but I've gotten far better about taking his length. I love the sound he makes when I swallow him in my throat, and I do it now just to hear it. It's somewhere between a growl and a moan and he grips my hair to guide me deeper. "Naughty," he whispers, and if my mouth wasn't full of him, I'd grin.

Matthew slowly fucks my mouth and throat, taking his time. He likes to take his time, both to take his pleasure the way he likes it and to show me that I have no control. It works, and I'm already soaking wet. I may be dripping onto the floor. He lifts his balls into my mouth and I suck them the way he likes, hard and slow, using my tongue to swirl back and forth. "Good girl," he groans, pulling them back. I smile at him, and he reaches down and draws a finger along the line of my necklace. "I like the way that looks on you."

"I like the way it feels."

He smirks and spins me around so my pussy is pressed against his cock. "I think you're going to like the feeling of this more." His cock plunges in, and I moan. God, I never get tired of the way that first thrust feels. I'm full and perfect and right now with the way the ropes are tight between my legs, he feels even bigger, and each thrust causes delicious friction on my clit.

He stands still, using the ropes to pull me onto his cock, and the rhythmic rocking onto his cock is amazing. He's using my own body to fuck me, and I can't do anything about it. Familiar and exquisite heat spreads through me, the thought of my position and predicament always gets me close. And now that I'm hanging, nothing but the ropes he bound me with keeping me from falling, it's that much stronger.

My breath is coming in short gasps, and I can't seem to catch my breath. Matthew thrusts again and again and I have to come. "Please Master, may I come?" He likes it when I call him Master. He likes it so much that he's more likely to let me have an orgasm.

"You may," he says, grinning.

He pulls me onto his cock, and I go over the edge. It's a smooth, rippling orgasm that spreads from my pussy to my spine and out, sweet pleasure flaring and fading just as fast. "Thank you, Sir."

"You're welcome."

It feels different now that I'm wearing his collar. More intimate. More perfect. He stops fully inside me, and I moan louder. Suspended and impaled and collared and I don't think I've ever been happier in my life. "I love you, Sir."

He reaches out and brushes my face. "I

love you, Emma." There's a moment of perfect silence between us and then his wicked, dangerous smile appears. "And I hope you loved that orgasm because I'm going to take my time with you, and you won't have another one for a while."

I bite my lip, holding back a sassy comeback that will get me a spanking. "Thank you, Master."

Matthew grins. "Good girl." And he starts to fuck me again.

THE END

Author Biography

Penny Wylder writes just that-- wild romances. Happily Ever Afters are always better when they're a little dirty, so if you're looking for a page turner that will make you feel naughty in all the right places, jump right in and leave your panties at the door!

Other Books by Penny Wylder

BIG MAN

Filthy Boss

Her Dad's Friend

Rockstars F#*k Harder

The Virgin Intern

Her Dirty Professor

The Pool Boy

Get Me Off

Caught Together

Selling Out to the Billionaire

Falling for the Babysitter

Lip Service

Full Service

Expert Service

The Billionaire's Virgin

The Billionaire's Secret Babies

Her Best Friend's Dad

Own Me

The Billionaire's Gamble

Seven Days With Her Boss

Virgin in the Middle

The Virgin Promise

First and Last

Tease

Spread

Bang

Second Chance Stepbrother

Dirty Promise

Sext

Quickie

Bed Shaker

Deep in You

The Billionaire's Toy

Buying the Bride

Dating My Friend's Daughter